THE MUTANT AND THE MULE

AA Blair

THE MUTANT AND THE MULE

Histria SciFi & Fantasy
Las Vegas ♦ Chicago ♦ Palm Beach

Published in the United States of America by
Histria Books,
7181 N. Hualapai Way, Ste. 130-86
Las Vegas, NV 89166 USA
HistriaBooks.com

Histria SciFi & Fantasy is an imprint of Histria Books encompassing outstanding, innovative works in the genres of science fiction and fantasy. Titles published under the imprints of Histria Books are distributed worldwide.

All rights reserved. No part of this book may be reprinted or reproduced or utilized in any form or by any electronic, mechanical or other means, now known or hereafter invented, including photocopying and recording, or in any information storage or retrieval system, without the permission in writing from the Publisher.

This is a work of fiction. Names, characters, places, and incidents either are the product of the author's imagination or are used fictitiously, and any resemblance to actual persons, living or dead, business establishments, events, or locales is entirely coincidental.

Library of Congress Control Number: 2024948885

ISBN 978-1-59211-532-7 (paperback)
ISBN 978-1-59211-548-8 (eBook)

Copyright © 2025 by A.A. Blair

AA Blair

THE MUTANT AND THE MULE

Histria SciFi & Fantasy
Las Vegas ♦ Chicago ♦ Palm Beach

Published in the United States of America by
Histria Books,
7181 N. Hualapai Way, Ste. 130-86
Las Vegas, NV 89166 USA
HistriaBooks.com

Histria SciFi & Fantasy is an imprint of Histria Books encompassing outstanding, innovative works in the genres of science fiction and fantasy. Titles published under the imprints of Histria Books are distributed worldwide.

All rights reserved. No part of this book may be reprinted or reproduced or utilized in any form or by any electronic, mechanical or other means, now known or hereafter invented, including photocopying and recording, or in any information storage or retrieval system, without the permission in writing from the Publisher.

This is a work of fiction. Names, characters, places, and incidents either are the product of the author's imagination or are used fictitiously, and any resemblance to actual persons, living or dead, business establishments, events, or locales is entirely coincidental.

Library of Congress Control Number: 2024948885

ISBN 978-1-59211-532-7 (paperback)
ISBN 978-1-59211-548-8 (eBook)

Copyright © 2025 by A.A. Blair

For daughters, especially mine.

CHAPTER 1

The sound of Helia's pounding heart filled her ears. The tiny hairs on her neck stood at attention, receptors for danger. They helped Helia sense the slightest movement, protecting her from unwanted surprises. This was the first time she had been inside a Norm compound. Over the past few months, Helia studied every map available in the encampment. Despite her familiarity with every nook and cranny of the Norm territory, she couldn't escape the sinking feeling of doubt. Could she trust their accuracy? Helia hugged the wall as she crept further. She was officially a mole. And she would be exterminated if discovered by the Department of Sanitation. Helia struggled to isolate the noises that swirled around her as she crept through the gloom. The sound, smell, and light could never be replicated in a simulation. Theory never worked as well as practical experience. It was challenging to translate two dimensional layouts to physical walls that danced with shadows like the bonfires she longed for back home. The phantom shapes jutted out at her, and Helia flinched, showing her anxiety as she reacted to the attacking shadows.

Helia felt ashamed of her fear. She was a trained Infiltrator sent on a mission to bring down the Norm compound. Phase one of the operation was to pose as a Norm herself and meet her inside contact. It was a fate she was born into; one she had been groomed to fulfill. Helia would have been considered quite beautiful by Norm standards. Her auburn hair flowed like a wild mane. Her slender body was that of a trained mercenary: long, lanky, sinewy muscle ready to attack if the occasion required. Just shy of her nineteenth birthday, Helia wore the typical garb of a childbearing Norm female. *Some present,* she thought to herself. The long, flowing skirt tugged at her skin and kept getting caught on the imperfections of the cold cement walls. She hated it, longing for her sleek battle suit concealed underneath.

Helia was an expert at Norm infiltration… in theory. By the end of her training, she could complete any of the simulations with her eyes closed. But things were different now. The simulations were just a game. Winning or losing was the extent of the danger. Now, on the inside, her life was at stake. People were counting on her to succeed. People she cared about. If Helia was discovered, everyone in her encampment would be in danger. The sparkling blue of Emily's eyes seeped into Helia's consciousness. Their tearful parting. Em's unborn child. Helia knew the stakes. They formed a mass of apprehension that sat in the pit of her stomach. This was no game.

Helia was to arrive at a mutant-sympathetic establishment. She was equipped with a blade for close combat and a .22 caliber zip gun that held two shots if she needed them. Her fingertips were capped with wax with a small packet of Norm blood under each slender finger. She needed this, just in case she was stopped by a Department of Sanitation Officer or had to pass through a checkpoint that required Norm clearance. Helia was also equipped with a passport and enough currency of the Americas to last her a month. She longed to shed her dress and let her battle suit blanket her under the comfortable cover of the shadows. But Helia forced herself to straighten and walk with the loathsome swagger she had practiced. It was a sickening throwback to the conservative Norm world. The walk was the worst part of her training. The echoes of laughter from her fellow soldiers rang in her ears. Helia smiled at the memory. She hated it at the time. Now she longed for the company of her comrades, but she was alone. The destruction of cellular tech in the early days of the war had completely cut Helia off from her unit.

Passing through the long corridors of alleys, Helia tried to calm her nerves. *Take deep breaths*, she told herself. The stale air of the domed compound choked her. During her training, Helia was warned that she would need to adjust. She spent hours with Troy, her operator, pouring over lists of preparations. But they were just lists. She often daydreamed while listening to him drone on. Mostly thinking about the different ways she could end his life. But now her mind raced, trying to remember all those things Troy had made her repeat, hoping they were lodged somewhere in her subconscious. The thought of Troy was usually enough to make her blood boil, but now she'd welcome his monotonous voice. Helia looked up at the rounded sky of the Norm compound. The artificial glare of the sun bathed the city in a pallid light, but it lacked the unfiltered warmth she always found comforting back home. Helia had opposed a mid-day infiltration, but Troy convinced her that the city would be more susceptible to an intrusion during a shift change rather than at night when there was heavier security.

Helia emerged from the maze of alleyways. She paused, taking in the entirety of the Norm compound known as Cincuenta Yuno. As one of the wealthiest and most densely populated Norm compounds, it boasted over two million inhabitants, most of whom were Norms. Cincuenta Yuno controlled two-thirds of the total wealth of the Unified Americas. It had the broadest range of classes and was a melting pot for both Mules and Norms. Cincuenta Yuno was the ideal Norm compound to hit. If they could gain control, the rest of the Unified Americas would be considerably weakened — an advantage that would give all Freeborns a sorely needed edge in the ongoing war. Helia studied the street she was on. By digesting the surrounding landmarks, Helia quickly correlated the visual data with the maps stored in her photographic memory. She turned north and walked with purpose toward her destination. She didn't want to stand out. Tourism was uncommon, and a look of uncertainty would draw the type of attention she wanted to avoid.

Helia was already concerned that she would have difficulty blending in with the population. Unlike most of its inhabitants, her skin had been touched by the sun's rays. Cincuenta Yuno's treated dome prevented the harmful agents hidden beneath the sun's warm rays. The dulling of the sun had drained the color from the faces of its citizens. Every attempt was made to ensure Helia would blend in with the pallid masses. She had to avoid the sun during certain times of the day. Helia looked forward to the passing seasons that promised more freedom and dreaded those that would add to her confinement. The thought of the pre-war era lotions she was forced to lather on made her nauseous. Helia did everything she could to scrub herself free from the sticky saccharine syrup before her mission. But the substance was burned into her nasal cavity. When she licked the nervous perspiration off her lips, she could still taste the medicinal sweetness — as if the lotion had taken up permanent residence in her pores. Helia looked nervously at the pedestrians that littered the street. She tried to read their faces to see whether she stuck out as much as she felt.

The pedestrians of Cincuenta Yuno didn't pay particular attention to Helia. Once she was close enough to steal the eyes of any onlookers, Helia's ears rang with jeering.

"That's right. Keep moving, sister."

"Find your own block; this one's taken!"

The onset of *The Change* affected women deeply. The ability to give birth to Norm babies became a commodity. Surrogate mothering became a business, one that had grown over the decades. If unable to birth a Norm child, most parents could browse catalogs or visit retail locations to choose a surrogate mother. However, freelancers emerged when surrogates realized greater profits could be had without big business taking a stake. It worked both ways. One could cruise the streets of Cincuenta Yuno and find a freelancer at a much cheaper rate, but there were more risks. To put a prospective investor's mind at ease, freelancers would often carry some credentials. The irony wasn't lost on Helia. In the Freelands, things weren't much better for women. Women who didn't have extraordinary powers were relegated to being concubines for the most powerful soldiers. They were applauded for doing their *duty*. Women of the Freelands and Cincuenta Yuno were bonded by the same oppression under the mantle of different propaganda. Helia's mind meandered to the memory of the gentle kick of Em's unborn. She *so* wanted to be happy for her. But Em's pregnancy was the end of their future. Helia had extraordinary talents — it's why she could remain a soldier. Emily wasn't as lucky. The thought of Emily performing her *duty* with Troy made Helia's veins course with anger. Helia quickly caught herself. She couldn't let herself be distracted. A wandering mind was dangerous for a soldier.

Helia kept running the gauntlet of threatening comments, not slowing her pace, lest she give herself away as an outsider. She heard the honks and hollers of passersby looking to make an *investment*. Helia navigated through the rows of angry, pale faces. She refocused on her mission. She was to arrive at Helena Tavern at twenty hundred hours. Helia was to rendezvous with Hector, a Norm bartender and the owner of the Freeland sympathetic establishment. By her estimates, it was close to sixteen hundred hours. Nonetheless, Helia thought it prudent to locate the establishment early. She briskly strolled through the streets, striding as confidently as possible toward her destination. Her eyes darted about, taking in every detail of the Norm compound.

The streets of Cincuenta Yuno were overcast. Ominous towers engulfed the city in premature darkness. The buildings were faceless monoliths. They stood at attention, guarding the streets below. The opaque veneer made it impossible to

detect if any eyes were watching from within. Helia recalled the stories: citizens of Cincuenta Yuno would flock to these monoliths, where they spent day after day imprisoned, forced to perform menial activities that — despite their insignificance — were framed as "integral to the ongoing success of their society." The brutalist architecture of gray jutting concrete further impressed upon Helia the notion of imprisonment. Cincuenta Yuno was consumed by a constant hum. Helia knew this to be their artificial climate. She would pass vents in the street that blew stale manufactured air into the domed bell jar. Helia had memorized the elaborate network of ducts that ran through Cincuenta Yuno like veins. Despite her eidetic memory, Helia obsessed over the maps. She traced her finger throughout the maze, wanting to learn every nuance of the complex duct system, imagining her passage through them. Helia knew that the ducts would be her only hope of escape if she were discovered.

Helia turned sharply onto the street where Helena Tavern was located. Her eyes darted across the faces of the Cincuenta Yuno pedestrians, looking for anyone suspicious. She wanted to be sure she wasn't being followed. Helia didn't see anything untoward, so she decided to rely on her other senses. She closed her eyes and took a deep breath, letting the stale air fill her nostrils. Helia's talents included the ability to detect pheromones, allowing her to know when someone was frightened, aroused, enraged, or ready to attack. It was a wonderful defense mechanism, but not without its drawbacks. Of all her abilities, being able to tell when her fellow soldiers — or worse, her commanding officers — got ideas was the most difficult to navigate. With Emily, Helia found herself racked with guilt, having an unfair advantage in their relationship. A smile crossed Helia's lips as she remembered Emily's response to her confession. "I don't care. I have nothing to hide. I want you to know how I feel." It was so different than the cat-and-mouse game Helia had been accustomed to playing. Helia's lips tightened. Any memory of Emily was accompanied with a pang of remorse. She scolded herself for the distraction and lack of focus. She snapped back to the moment. Processing the information her nose had taken in, Helia was confident that no one in the immediate vicinity was on to her. She proceeded confidently down Leuctra Drive.

Leuctra Drive was a portal to another time. A forgotten alley that harkened back to the pre-war era. The buildings weren't the uniform monoliths that towered over Cincuenta Yuno. It was a collage of architecture. The buildings were woven together. All different shapes and sizes, colorful and unique. Despite their vibrance, Helia could tell that these buildings were neglected by comparison. The sanitary coolness of the Norm towers would never abide the visible wear, filth, and signs of life. Helia knew she was in a Mule district.

Mules were the result of Mutant/Norm interbreeding. They were sterile and did not have as long a life expectancy as either Mutants or Norms. Helia's studies taught her that Mules were responsible for the majority of manual labor required to run Cincuenta Yuno. Norms tended to revile Mules. They considered them a servant class. Mules were provided segregated living quarters, which rejuvenated the pre-war districts.

Mules didn't possess any Mutant abilities, but they tended to be stronger than the average Norm. For this reason, Mules had a place in Norm society. They were not exiled like Mutants. They were not the enemy. They were not a threat. Norms employed Mules to perform labor that required physical strength or put the worker in significant physical danger. Mules were required to wear fluorescent orange jumpsuits that were standard government issue. They were not educated and were considered expendable by the Norms. Mules often suffered from substance abuse and had a high rate of suicide. The rendezvous in the Mule district was by design. There would be less Norm traffic, and Mules wouldn't care who she was. The site was ideal for their purpose. It mitigated the mountain of risk that loomed over the operation.

Helia admired the character they had infused into their little alley of the Norm compound. The Mules compensated for the monotony of their existence by adding life to their surroundings. The storefronts were warmly decorated with relics from the pre-war era. Anything with an opaque surface was colorfully painted. Walls were bright and cheerful, while roofs tended to be deeper contrasting colors. Slogans like "Drink till you Drop" and "Feel Supa Walkin' Down Leuctra" were posted in store windows to entice patronage from passersby. Helia was impressed by how the Mules created a feeling of warmth in the most impassive places.

Helia counted the numbers of each building, stopping abruptly as she neared her destination. Helena's Tavern was boarded up with a sign reading, "Closed by the Department of Sanitation." Helia tried to suppress a gasp as she approached the quarantined establishment. Her heart began to race at the prospect of what it could mean to her mission. The Department of Sanitation must have discovered that it was a Freeland-sympathetic establishment. Helia forgot her training. She panicked. Her mission was compromised, and she was shaken by the uncertainty. Her training would have told her to stay on the move, remain composed, and find a safe spot to regroup. She knew that the compromised location may be under surveillance. She was right, although she didn't know it yet. Eyes were watching Helena Tavern, and judging by Helia's actions, they had just found what they had been looking for.

***

Francis had been on the Department of Sanitation force for just six months. He was a wide-eyed rookie who wanted to make a difference. He still had idealism. A pride that had him polishing the embossed Department of Sanitation emblem on his poly-carbonite armor after every shift. The clenched fist surrounded by a wheel had meant a lot to Francis. His father had worked for the Department of Sanitation, and his father's father was an officer in the pre-war era. When Francis looked at the polished emblem, he imagined it was *his* fist. *His* might that kept the wheels of justice turning.

Like most rookies, Francis was relegated to beat duty. He would cruise the streets to ensure the freelancers were registered, not being abused, or not with child and continuing to work. The Norm future depended on a constant supply of Norm babies. After the horrible cloning experiments, surrogates had become the most reliable method of rearing Norm children. His mission was to protect Norms and ensure that any Mutie filth was exterminated. This surveillance assignment was his first chance to prove that he was Seeker material. Seekers were responsible for covert operations in the Freelands. They hunted down Mutie communities and "sanitized" them. The Mutie terror *had* to be eliminated.

It was Francis' first stakeout. A few weeks back, Helena Tavern had been busted for Mutant-sympathetic activities. The owner and bartender, Hector, had been brought in for interrogation — he didn't survive. Under the duress of torture, Hector had confessed to his Mutie sympathies. Francis heard that Hector had a Mutie uncle or something to that effect. He was scheduled to meet an Infiltrator in the coming weeks. Thinking of Norms like Hector made Francis sick to his stomach. To sell out one's own people for some idealistic Mutie propaganda was enough to make him puke.

Francis had been put on the op with his lazy partner, John. John had been on the force for the past ten years; he was a seasoned veteran. He was in his late thirties, and his jet-black hair had practically disappeared. He was overweight, and his polycarbonate armor creaked under his carriage. Francis wasn't fond of John. He didn't trust him. Anyone who wasn't serious enough to keep in shape couldn't be counted on in the line of fire. The department heads must have realized the same thing since John had never performed any Seeker duties and remained an officer. Francis listened to John gurgle as he snored, trying to stay as alert as possible while he watched Helena's Tavern.

Francis decided he'd take on any co-conspirators himself. He wouldn't wake up John and put his life in the hands of a bungling idiot. People like John should be exposed, not given a free ride. Francis wasn't about to share his success. A win would help speed along his dream of becoming a Seeker. Francis eyed the tavern intently, wishing for something to happen. His glare dared anyone to give him an excuse to jump into action. From the corner of his eye, he caught a hint of movement. A young woman possibly in her mid-twenties approached. She was a vision of beauty — her auburn hair flowed past her shoulders. She wore the typical flowing skirt of a surrogate. The fabric still clung just enough to show off an athletic figure beneath. A drop of sweat trickled from his forehead to his lips, awakening him from his trance.

The woman stopped. She looked lost. Her head swiveled, searching for something. Francis realized he should be watching Helena's Tavern, but he couldn't help himself. Francis had lost himself in the moment. He was disoriented. Scanning the area to regain his bearings, he realized that "Helena's Tavern" framed the figure that had distracted him. Francis smiled to himself. Now Francis could watch the woman and the tavern at the same time. She had a beautiful face; a smooth sloping forehead that led to a button nose. Her eyes were big and wide. They glistened a bright hazel. Her lips twisted with confusion. Francis thought about getting out and asking if she needed help. She must have been lost. After all, what would a Norm woman be doing in a Mule district? Come to think of it, what *would* a Norm woman be doing standing in front of Helena's Tavern, looking confused and distraught? His heart sank. She must have been their target. How could she be involved with any Mutie filth? His remorse was overtaken by a hot flash of anger. How could he let himself be deceived? He was going to make her pay. Make her pay for taking his attention away from his priority. Make her pay for conspiring with Mutie scum. Francis decided she wasn't going to live to testify. He was going to take her out quickly. John was asleep, so there would be no witnesses. He'd plant a weapon on her to make it look necessary. He'd be a hero and be rewarded with a Seeker opportunity. Francis opened the door to the vehicle that was nestled into a narrow alley. His black armor blended into the shadows cast by the pre-war buildings, concealing the light from the slowly setting sun. He crept stealthily toward his unsuspecting target. The streets were silent as he focused on his prey. His mouth twisted into a bloodthirsty smile. He licked his lips in anticipation as he got closer, muscles coiling as he prepared to pounce.

She doesn't have a prayer, he thought to himself.

***

Helia couldn't believe that Helena's Tavern had been compromised. It was her only checkpoint. Without Hector, she didn't know what she was going to do. It wasn't part of the plan, and there was no backup. Her vulnerability surrounded her. She was exposed on all sides. She was going to have to return to camp. The mission was a failure. Helia looked up and down the street, hoping for a sign. She needed answers, some direction, a next step. Helia's head raced with ideas. Maybe she didn't have to flee. She could continue posing as a freelancer until an opportunity presented itself. She had enough money to last a month and all the necessary papers. Maybe she could lay low and blend in — at least for a while. The only difficulty was she couldn't contact her operator for specifics. Mobile communications and networks had been taken down as part of the war measures. Social applications were dissolved. They proved too risky —factions could easily mobilize and launch an insurrection. Helia wasn't even aware of her mission specifics. Hector had those details. Ops were never shared with an Infiltrator, lest they be discovered. Infiltrators could be replaced, but inside contacts could not. The ideas bombarded her: maybe *she* could make sympathetic connections; there had to be others in the Mule district. If Troy and Hector were in communication, there must be a way for her to get a message back to camp. Her thought process was interrupted by the minute hairs on her neck standing on end. There was movement behind her. Helia's faculties were assaulted by the pheromones of rage.

Helia could feel her attacker closing in. She leaped into a cartwheel kick. Helia's boot caught a surprised Francis in the chin — the crunch of his teeth shattering from the force rang in her ears. As she twisted in the air, her eyes met her victim. A Department of Sanitation officer. His body armor and gleaming emblem were all too familiar from her training. She landed and quickly leaped again, attempting another strike. Francis avoided the blow. Helia contorted without touching the ground, concentrating on gathering all the loose matter around her. Air particles, dust, sound, anything she could use. The vortex that engulfed the two combatants became silent. Debris drew toward her like a magnet. Francis lunged consumed with rage. He tried to time a tackle with her landing. As Helia touched the ground, she saw his attempt to overwhelm her with brute force. But Helia was calm in the face of her foe, who gnashed his broken teeth like a rabid animal. She felt the power of the loose matter gather into her, and with a deafening crack, she released it into his chest. The matter exploding into Francis hit him like a grenade and stopped his heart immediately.

In the instant before his heart stopped, Francis realized that this was his first encounter with a Mutant. It would also be his last. Helia watched the expression of shock on his face. Her aim for the emblem of the Department of Sanitation was true, and she watched as his limbs convulsed in their death throes. Helia staggered. A matter blast always took so much out of her. It was like standing up too quickly. She was temporarily blinded by a bright light. Slowly the brightness ebbed away to reveal reality.

She looked at her victim. It was her first Norm kill. She had done many simulations, but this was the first time she had killed someone. Helia felt nauseous. She didn't know this man. He was just doing his job like she was. She felt a pang of guilt but quickly scolded herself for it. As Helia attempted to regain her composure, she felt a sudden sharp pain vibrate up her spine. She lost control of her limbs as she hit the ground, engulfed in darkness.

***

CRACK!

The loud noise woke John from his slumber. Although John was a large man, he swiftly grabbed his taser and rolled out of the car into a crouch in one smooth motion. He peered over the hood of the car to assess the scene. He saw his partner sprawled awkwardly on the ground. John knew at first glance that Francis was dead. He had seen or been responsible for enough deaths during his tour of duty with the Department of Sanitation. John scanned his surroundings and saw that the killer seemed to be an unarmed freelancer. The melee had happened in front of Helena's Tavern. John immediately concluded that the woman must be a Mutant. There was no other explanation for a Norm woman to be standing over the carcass of a Department of Sanitation officer. John cursed the rookie for not waking him. It could have saved his life. As a unit, they had a chance to apprehend a Mutant, but in single combat, it was unlikely. John knew that Francis didn't like him. He knew that Francis thought he was a lazy and overweight embodiment of a pre-war law-enforcement stereotype. But John had been on the force for over ten years and knew a thing or two about staying alive. John was about to retreat and call in for assistance when he realized he had a shot at the Mutant. She was staggering and disoriented. John reacted quickly. Springing from his crouch behind his vehicle, he rolled over the hood and lunged at the woman. He only needed to get within five feet to immobilize her with his taser. As he landed in front of his vehicle, John fluidly aimed his taser and stuck the back of the neck of the unsuspecting Mutant. She stiffened and collapsed in convulsions.

John reevaluated the scene. He estimated that he had at least a couple of hours before the Mutant came to. It was only a guess. John had only witnessed a taser's effect on rogue Norms and Mules. He'd never taken down a Mutant before. He wound up the taser and put it into his side holster. The taser was a weapon used by most street officers in the department. Most of the heavy artillery was reserved for the Seekers. The department had decided they didn't want their street officers armed with heavy artillery. The optics were bad. They didn't want to give the impression that they were a military state ruled by force. That usually made the general population uneasy. It also ensured that street officers would take prisoners, which was always more valuable to the department. The interrogation techniques of the Department of Sanitation were renowned for their effectiveness, but it required live prisoners.

Of course, the Department of Sanitation officers didn't roam the streets of Cincuenta Yuno only armed with a taser. They did have concealed weaponry, but their use was discouraged. Months of inquiries and inquests would ensue if they used their more lethal weapons, not to mention the paperwork. The taser was the weapon of choice; it had a good range and only needed to slightly touch skin to send enough voltage through a victim's body to take them down. They weren't foolproof devices; they had been known to kill. But on the whole, they were an effective means of immobilization and detention.

John looked over at his ex-partner and sneered. He didn't want him dead, but he knew Francis would have been in complete shock if he were still alive and witnessed that John had done the very thing that had cost Francis his life. The shame would've killed Francis, even if the Mutant didn't. But John wasn't without remorse for his lost partner. Francis was young. He had aspirations and drive; a bright future. But it was also his youth and enthusiasm that made him a risk. He acted without thinking. A combination that endangered himself and his colleagues. It was the cause of his death. The Department of Sanitation training did what it could to stamp out the behavior. Francis should've followed his training and woken his partner. John's veteran eye could've assessed the situation and given them a plan of action that would've made them heroes. Instead, the Department had lost an officer in the line of duty — something rare.

John shook his head and looked at the collapsed Mutant woman on the ground. On the one hand, her capture would make him a hero, but on the other hand, losing a partner would make him a pariah. Losing a partner in the Department wasn't taken lightly. It could ruin an officer. Teammates were supposed to protect their other halves. Even though Francis didn't have the sense to wake John, John would still be scorned by his peers and commanding officers. This violated a sacred trust. Looking at Francis, John couldn't choke back his contempt for his dead partner. The glory-grubbing bastard got himself killed and made John a failure in the process. John returned his gaze to the Mutant. His rage burned. She was the perfect target for his anger. He decided he would get his licks in before handing her over. Walking over to the Mutant, he grabbed a handful of her auburn hair. John pulled her head up and punched her. Seeing both the Mutant and Francis' faces, he repeatedly punched until a clump of hair ripped out of his hand. The Mutant's skull hit the street with a thud. John's rage didn't subside. His anger toward the situation consumed him. Consumed with blood lust, he was going to kill her with his bare hands, screw the consequences.

***

CRACK!

The loud noise woke Ari. She peeled her face from a pool of her own vomit. She had passed out again after drinking too much. Ari skipped work that day. She did it as often as possible because Ari knew she wouldn't be fired. After all, who else would do her job? It wasn't like it was her career by choice. She didn't *have* a choice. She was a Mule, born into a life of doing Norms' dirty work. Ari had heard fables of Mules passing as Norms, using elaborate schemes of counterfeit eyes and blood. Ari was skeptical. She had never met a Mule who passed as a Norm, but maybe that was the point. She doubted they would reveal themselves to her, but if Ari didn't see it, she didn't believe it. That sort of thing wasn't for her. All Ari wanted was to do her job and get trashed, which was fitting considering her line of work. Ari managed waste. She spent long hours in Cincuenta Yuno's elaborate sewage systems. Her job was to ensure that the sewage didn't bottleneck at any point. Ari was also responsible for monitoring the levels of harmful pollutants. She took various readings of sewage with a machine that performed calculations and stored the data. Ari would dock the device to the mainframe when she returned to the office to upload the statistics. She had heard it referred to as a "retro set-up" by some of the elder Mules, who spoke of a time when downloading or uploading (she always got those two confused) could be done from the comfort of one's home. But Ari never knew differently. The fabled days of wireless connections and access to information were long outlawed by the Norm ruling class. Ari didn't care about the readings, what they were for, or what the results were. She knew what she had to do, when to do it, and when it was over so she could go to the bar. Ari's life began when she got to the bar. Or so she thought.

Since the closure of her favorite establishment, Helena's Tavern, Ari often woke up in her current state. Hector, the owner, and bartender, usually put up with Ari enough that he would let her sleep off whatever damage she had done to herself in his office. The result wouldn't be much different, but at least she was comfortable. Now that Helena's Tavern had been shut down, Ari attempted to find a home at other Mule establishments. But none of the neighboring proprietors had the same patience for her. Ari had been banned from every liquor-serving Mule establishment in Cincuenta Yuno. The only remaining options for her to attempt were Norm bars. But Ari knew she couldn't walk into one of those in her government-issued fluorescent orange jumpsuit. She would be laughed out — or worse — end up waking up on the street in her own pool of blood, which was much worse than vomit. The only way Ari could get into a Norm establishment was by those tricks of fake blood and eyes, and she just felt the effort wasn't worth it. Even if she wanted to, Ari wouldn't know where to start, who to contact, or have the money to pull it off. So, she went to the local vendor, purchased her own liquor, and wandered the Mule district drinking by herself. It usually ended in an altercation with another Mule, or Ari would eventually just black out and wake up as she just did. Well, almost. Today was unusual.

Bleary-eyed, Ari rose to her feet. She looked around to try and determine her coordinates. She was near her old watering hole, Helena's Tavern. Ari couldn't make out the noise's exact point of origin. It had flooded her senses entirely. The noise still echoed in her head. Ari was agitated. Still drunk and cranky from being woken up, she wanted to teach the culprit to be more mindful of other people. Ari then had a thought. They had closed Helena's. Tearing it down seemed like a logical next step. It would explain the noise. Ari decided to investigate. If Helena's was being torn down, she wasn't sure how she'd take it: by solemnly paying final respects or by chaining herself to the building.

Ari rounded the corner. She stopped in her tracks. In front of Helena's Tavern, a Department of Sanitation officer was brutally assaulting what appeared to be a Norm woman. The officer had the woman by her hair and was repeatedly punching her face. Her eyes had swollen shut, so the officer must have been working her over for a bit. He was going to kill her. Ari noticed another officer on the ground. His limbs were twisted unnaturally. He had to be dead. Ari began to creep closer, noticing that the dead officer's polycarbonate armor had collapsed around his chest. She had never seen anything do that to polycarbonate armor before. Ari jumped to the conclusion that the remaining live officer must have gone rogue. , or crazy from being the wrong corner of a love triangle. Or it was an insane psycho posing as an officer. The woman looked helpless and unarmed. She was going to be the next victim. Even if she was wrong, it was a good rationale for what Ari would do next. Plus, Ari never liked the Department of Sanitation and their officers.

Ari crept up behind the officer. He was so involved in his work that he had no idea Ari was there. She tapped him on the shoulder and he stiffened, motionless.

The officer grabbed at his taser and began to spin around. Ari had been zapped in the past. She wasn't interested in reliving the experience. Before he could complete his spin, Ari landed a crushing blow to his chin. The officer staggered, dropping his taser, as he tried to steady himself with his hands. Ari snatched up the weapon and fired up the voltage with a touch of a button. The officer regained his balance along with his bearings. A wave of realization passed his face.

"*Wait!*" but Ari just smiled and slammed the taser against his face. The officer's body writhed as the voltage coursed through him. He quickly lost consciousness and collapsed, landing with a resounding thud. Ari slipped the taser into the front pouch of her jumpsuit, deciding that it may come in handy down the road. Ari looked down at the woman who had been mercilessly beaten. She was still breathing, so she was alive, at least. That was a relief. Ari didn't want to risk a Department of Sanitation interrogation on a corpse. She hoisted the woman over her shoulder and began walking toward her apartment. Ari would get her bandaged up before involving any additional authorities. She wasn't entirely sure what had just transpired, and she was hoping that the woman could shed some light on the situation before she decided what to do next.

CHAPTER 2

Helia was woken by a warm moisture gently pressing against her face. Her memory rushed back. With a start, she tried to open her eyes and get to her feet. A slit of light penetrated the darkness and sent a sharp pain through her body. The sensation made Helia reel, and she fell back onto the soft surface beneath her. She was prone, helpless, and blind. But a voice comforted her.

"Easy there. You were roughed up a bit. You're gonna need some rest so you can strengthen up."

The voice was soothing. It was a woman's. Deep and raspy, Helia was tickled by its vibrations. She didn't sense any danger. She could feel the concern from her comforter. The last thing she remembered was killing the Department of Sanitation officer.

"What happened?" Helia asked.

"I was going to ask you the same question," the voice replied. "All I know is that I rounded the corner onto Leuctra and found a Department of Sanitation officer pounding on you."

"Damn, there was another one?! I'm so stupid. I should've known." Helia's response made her nurse uneasy.

"So…you killed that officer? I thought he must have gone ballistic — some kind of love triangle thing or a deal gone bad. You did that? I've never seen armor damaged like that?"

Helia realized she'd said too much. She let the feeling of safety get the better of her. All that training she went through was for naught. As soon as someone was kind to her, she let vital information slip out. For all she knew, this could've been a Norm ploy to get information out of her. She calmed herself and tried to salvage whatever remained of her innocence.

"You're right. It was a love triangle. They were fighting over me, and it got out of hand."

"C'mon now, don't lie to me. You just said that you didn't know there was another one. Don't worry, I'm not one of them. I'm a Mule. And I'm the gal who rescued you from getting beaten to death."

Helia flushed with relief. "Thank you."

"You're welcome, I think. But you still haven't answered my question: What happened? Why was that officer going to beat you to death? How did that other officer die?"

Helia thought about the question for a while. She knew she shouldn't tell this woman a thing, but her interrogation interrupted her thought process.

"I see your eyelids moving. I know you're thinking something up. I told you already you're safe. You're in my apartment."

Helia opened her mouth to respond, but nothing came out.

"Alright," the voice replied. "You don't have to tell me anything yet. Just concentrate on getting better. But I do expect an explanation later. I want to know what I've got myself into."

Helia relaxed. The stranger's voice trailed off, leaving Helia to her thoughts.

Helia felt her battered face. Her eyelids were swollen shut. Every nerve ending screamed at the slightest touch. There were open cuts on her lip. She couldn't imagine what she looked like. The stranger was right. The other officer must have really laid into her. She knew she wouldn't be laid up for long. She could feel her healing ability working overtime. Her wounds were closing, the swelling subsiding. She let her consciousness slip away. She had to figure out her next steps, and this stranger was her only contact in Cincuenta Yuno. The soothing voice was Helia's only hope to successfully complete her mission.

***

Ari returned to the sink, stunned and confused. She couldn't process the exchange she just had with her houseguest. *She didn't know that there was another officer?* The implications of that statement! Ari looked around at her kitchen. Her self-consciousness grew. It had been a while since it had been cleaned. Her apartment was above one of the Mule establishments in the district. It wasn't much to speak of. The walls were an off-white. Ari thought they were probably white at some point, but time and neglect had added a dingy hue to them. The ceilings were lined with cracks that looked like spiderwebs. The cracks spilled down the sides of the walls. The faux-walnut cupboards were peeling, revealing their wood chip core. The sink's faucet and knobs were rusted. They always allowed some water to escape when turned on, leaving a brown trail indicating the dripping routes. Ari *did* have a window that overlooked an alley. It doubled as an exit to her fire escape, though the fire escape looked more treacherous than any fire could be.

The floors of Ari's apartment were tiled gray, covered with a permanent film. A mixture of dust, grease, and miscellaneous stomped into a glossy veneer by neglect. Some of the tiles were missing, revealing the black tar that held the remaining squares in place. An off-white fridge rattled and hummed beside its partner: a matching stove that has grown, in time, to match the walls. The fridge door was always unbalanced and had to be lifted to close. The stove had four burners, only two of which worked. They were essentially an electric archeological exhibit and took an eternity to heat up. Any time Ari used them, she could smell the history of previously cooked meals whose residue remained on the charred coils. There was no doubt that some of the scents dated back to a time before she occupied the apartment. The stove was rarely used now. Ari's diet consisted of alcohol and whatever bar snacks were available at her watering hole. Ari was sure that apartments like hers could be found in Norm documentaries, relics of the pre-war era.

Ari turned on the sink, and the faucet performed its regular routine: jerking spasmodically. It shot out streams of brown sludge before clear water began to flow. Ari rinsed the tattered pink washcloth she had used to nurse her patient. She turned her patient's statement over in her head. "*There was another one. I'm so stupid. I should've known.*" What possible scenario could her patient have been in? Was she ripping off the officer, and the deal went bad? Any way she looked at it, this woman wasn't as much a victim as Ari had thought. *She* had killed that officer. Ari couldn't fathom how the diminutive Norm female could have pulled it off.

Ari made her way back into the living area, which continued the off-white motif. Her patient was lying on an old sofa that had come with the apartment. It was light brown with orange detailing. The synthetic material was horribly uncomfortable for the skin to touch. The upholstery had a rough, waffle-like texture that always left a mark when pressed against flesh. Ari wasn't too concerned about her shabby furniture. She was sure her patient's circumstances would insulate her from judgment. As she approached, Ari noticed that her patient didn't look half as bad as when she had first brought her into her apartment. The swelling around her eyes looked like it was subsiding. It no longer looked like her eyes were two slits cut into some bulging fruit. Her lips weren't as puffy, and blood had ceased flowing from the cuts. Her bruises, deep purple just a minute ago, had begun turning lighter and, in some places, had started to yellow. She couldn't believe her eyes. She placed the moist washcloth against her forehead and squeezed. The warm water spilled down her patient's forehead, making it crinkle. She opened her eyes, which were a striking hazel. Ari jumped to her feet. When she left for the kitchen, her patient's eyes were swollen shut. Now they were wide open, alert. Ari stumbled back, lost her balance, and hit the cold tiled floor.

***

Helia opened her eyes to see a stocky woman. Her features were worn, and the wrinkles around her eyes were full of experience. She had jet-black hair with eyes just as dark as if they were only pupils. Her complexion wasn't the same pallid hue of other inhabitants of the Norm compound. Her face was round, but her features were sharp and angular. Her lips were full but wrinkled at the sides. It showed a stern disposition with a strong jaw that clenched as she tried to process Helia. She was shaggy as if she hadn't cut her hair in months, and her stained orange jumpsuit confirmed that she was indeed a Mule. If this woman was an operate of the Department of Sanitation, she was deep undercover. No one could just slip into this disguise. It was authentic. The look of shock on her face was also telling. Helia could sense her anxiety building. Her pheromones secreted a mix of fear and surprise. Her thick eyebrows pushed up in shock. She fell backward and hit the floor, shaking the entire room. Helia knew she was safe with this woman.

Helia rose to her feet and bent over her. "Here, let me help you up."

She stammered, "Um, it's okay, don't worry about me. You shouldn't be on your feet. You should be — uh — resting so you can heal."

Helia didn't sit. Ari got to her feet. She was almost as short as she was wide. Ari wasn't obese, but like most Mules, she was very broad. At her standing height,

Ari only reached Helia's neck. They stood in silence. Their eyes met, and for an awkward moment, time paused as they stared and studied each other. Helia broke the tension with a smile.

Ari stumbled back, embarrassed. "Now that you're on your feet, I want some answers," she exclaimed, trying to gain her composure.

"What is your name?" Helia asked in a soothing voice.

"Ari," she replied.

"Thank you, Ari, for saving my life."

Ari felt herself blush. She tried to remain focused. "You're welcome. What's your name?"

"Helia."

"What happened back there?"

"I defended myself."

"Why were you attacked?"

"Because I looked suspicious."

"Did you kill that officer?"

"Yes"

"Why?"

"Because he would have killed me."

"How did you kill him?"

"With a matter blast."

"What?"

"You don't want to know."

"I wouldn't ask if I didn't! How come you're healing so quickly?"

"Because I'm a Mutant."

"Oh."

The staccato questioning ceased. Ari had never met a Mutant before. Helia was different from what Ari expected a Mutant would look like. Ari thought there'd be three heads, green skin, horns, or something. From descriptions she had heard and read, she didn't expect a Mutant to look so much like a regular Norm.

Ari continued, "How did you get inside?"

"Through the sewers, of course. How else?"

"Of course," Ari muttered. "Well, why are you here?" Ari asked.

"I'm a Freeborn. I've trained for this ever since I can remember. But to answer your question, I know *why* I'm here, but I don't know *what* I'm supposed to do."

"What does that mean?"

"I was set to rendezvous with a Mutant-sympathetic Norm named Hector, but it looks like the Department of Sanitation got to him first."

Ari's shoulders slouched. She let out a sigh.

"Hector was my friend. It's been tough without Helena's Tavern."

Helia began to prod. "Have you spoken with Hector? Do you know where he is?"

"No, I don't. One day after work, I went by Helena's, and it was closed. I haven't been inside or seen him since."

Helia believed her. She could feel Ari's loss. "I'm also lost without him," Helia said. "He was my only contact here. I was going to get my orders from him, and now I don't know my next move."

Ari frowned. Her dark, bushy eyebrows pushed together.

"What's wrong?" Helia asked.

"It just occurred to me that Hector is probably dead. Or if he isn't, he probably wishes he was."

Helia matched Ari's frown. Ari was right. Helena's Tavern was shut down because of Hector's correspondence with the Freelands. Their communications must have been intercepted. Helia knew the rumors. Hector would be tortured until he revealed what they wanted to know. Even worse, that wasn't always the end of Norm "traitors." More unspeakable acts could ensue once their usefulness had passed. The Department of Sanitation certainly wasn't wasteful. They were rumored to perform ghastly experiments whenever they finished with a captive. The stories often circulated amongst the Freelands, breeding fear.

Helia placed a hand on Ari's shoulder. "I'm sorry for your loss."

Ari nodded. She knew that there was nothing she could do about Hector now. Ari was officially friendless. She worked in relative isolation, had been banned from most pubs in the Mule districts, and was estranged from her family at birth. She was a Mule. Raised by the government to perform the tasks that none of the Norms wanted. Ari smiled.

Helia, noticing her sudden change of disposition, asked, "Are you alright? Is there something I'm missing?"

Ari looked at her with a menacing grin, eyes twinkling with the hint of an idea. Helia sensed Ari was becoming erratic. She braced herself for the worst. Maybe Ari was a Department of Sanitation officer after all, and Helia had just been caught in the dragnet. Had Helia been tricked into telling them everything?

"Tell me what you're thinking," Helia pleaded, preparing to strike Ari if needed.

"I know you don't know me," Ari began, "but Hector was pretty much my only friend. The Department has taken him away for trying to help Muties. I know I haven't done anything for anyone, but if Hector thought he should be helping Muties, then I guess I should too."

Helia sighed. "That's good to know," she confessed.

"The best way to honor Hector is by finishing what he started."

Helia smiled. "You've just made a second friend."

Ari returned it with a warmer, friendlier smile. The psychotic determination faded from her face. "All the more reason to help you," she winked.

"Well, where do we start?" Helia asked eagerly.

Ari sat down again and leaned back on the floor, revealing her strong shoulders and chest. Helia could tell that Ari was a very powerful woman.

Ari replied nonchalantly, lying back on her elbows, "We break into Helena's Tavern."

Helia frowned. She feared that Ari's enthusiasm and strength might not be matched with brains.

"How are we going to do that? Did you kill the other officer?"

"No," Ari responded.

"Then he's definitely reported it. If Hector didn't already tell them, they'll now know a Freeborn infiltration has occurred. And since Helena's Tavern was where it happened, I'm sure they'll be watching non-stop."

"Listen, I have access to the sewers. We'll be able to get into Helena's that way. We'll slip in when they're not looking. They'll never expect you to break in using the sewage system."

"Why not?" Helia asked. "That's how I got in!"

Ari paused and thought for a moment. The tension between them grew with their silence. Ari took a deep breath and began to speak, "Look, Helia, I don't see how we have any other options. I could give you my Mule uniform, which might disguise you for a while, but it won't last. You don't look like a Mule," Ari gestured at her, highlighting their differences in appearance. "You'll have to trust me — I work in the sewers all day, and I've never seen a Norm down there. Why do you think I'm there? Because a Norm wouldn't be caught dead wading through crap. They won't be ready for it because they don't think of the sewers, period. They leave that to us Mules. Even if they do catch us, we can retreat into the sewers. No one knows the sewers like me. Anyway, if you don't do anything, they'll track you down sooner or later. And you can't spend the rest of your days here. You came here to complete your mission. Hector isn't around to give you your orders, so I'm offering my help to get into Hector's place and get the orders he would've given you."

Helia softened. "How do you know the orders haven't already been found by the Department?"

Ari smiled — she knew she was gaining ground. "Hector had a very secret and secure hiding spot for his valuables. I know he'd die before telling the Department about it. He would've made something up to satisfy them and stop the torture. He knew he was dead anyway, so why prolong the process by trying to hide something he wasn't about to give up?"

"And if he didn't?"

"Well, we get caught and get killed. It's going to happen either way. Even if your mission *is* a success, it's suicidal. I don't know how anyone would have thought you'd successfully infiltrate and live."

Helia became defensive. "I came here to become a Norm infiltrator on the inside."

Ari laughed. "That's what they told you, but I don't see how that would help. And what would it accomplish? You didn't know your orders for a reason."

Helia frowned. Ari suddenly made a lot of sense for someone she didn't think was too bright a few seconds ago. "I don't know, Ari. It sounds risky to me." She hadn't contemplated the operation being a suicide mission. All soldiers know this is a possibility, an exchange for the greater good. But hearing Ari say it so matter-of-factly hit Helia. Her thoughts went to Emily. The realization that she may never see her again. Never meet her child. Helia's jaw clenched, thinking of Troy. This was a perfect way to eliminate Helia from their new lives as parents.

Ari smiled. "I know it's suicidal. That's why it'll work. Because it's crazy."

Helia looked at Ari. She could feel the adrenaline-induced aggression. Helia couldn't help but be affected.

"Alright. We're short on options," Helia relented.

"Well," Ari said, "we have some planning to do. I'll explore the sewage systems that pass under Helena's Tavern tomorrow while you heal up here. You're gonna need your health when we break in. I'll draw some maps up. You think you can learn them quickly?"

Helia smiled. "I have an eidetic memory, don't worry,"

"An eye-den-tik what?" Ari asked.

Helia rephrased. "A photographic memory. All you have to do is show it to me once, and I'll remember it."

Ari blushed at her ignorance. "We'll be ready even sooner then."

CHAPTER 3

Franco DeSouza pounded his desk in fury. He had a mole on his hands. It was the first one since his term as Director of the Department of Sanitation. He snatched the report off his desk and looked closely at its author.

"Get Officer John Harris in front of me now," he bellowed into an intercom connected to his assistant. "Hey, did you get that?" the director yelled.

"Yes, Director DeSouza," was the crackling response.

"Good," DeSouza muttered under his breath. He threw the report back on his desk while he awaited the arrival of John Harris. Director DeSouza was in his early fifties. He was a tall, slender man. His Caribbean complexion had faded over the years of living under a dome, revealing dark freckles across the bridge of his nose. The director's hair was gray, but there were dark patches that showed that it was once black. His features were soft, and his eyes were big and brown, weathered by crow's feet. He had a rounded flat nose with a slightly crooked bridge from being broken numerous times during his career. DeSouza was once a beat officer, just like John Harris, and had worked his way up to being a director through hard work and many late nights. He earned the respect of his officers, and he was usually on their side, but today was different.

Not more than twenty-four hours earlier, Cincuenta Yuno had been infiltrated by Mutie scum. The Mutant had made its way into the Mule district. *It must have been through the sewage systems*, DeSouza thought to himself. DeSouza had posted officers in response to Hector the Mutie-sympathetic traitor's apprehension. Contrary to Hector's confessions — the Mutie-sympathetic traitor — a Mutant *did* show up at his establishment. DeSouza knew Hector was a lying bastard. DeSouza decided to post two officers at Helena's Tavern instead of drones. That way, if a Mutie did show up, he had the forces to apprehend it and bring it in for questioning. He didn't want it terminated without learning more about the Mutie plans. The infiltration happened off-shift, so Hector must have been feeding the Mutants good information. Too bad the information he gave the department during his interrogation wasn't of the same caliber. What infuriated DeSouza most was that he was empty-handed. His hunch was correct, but the Mutie had escaped and killed one of its bright young officers, Francis Baisley. Francis reminded DeSouza of himself so many years ago. Determined, enthusiastic — director material. DeSouza knew that Francis would be vying for his job within a decade. That's why he liked him. After all, DeSouza was one of the youngest to make Director in the department's history. DeSouza thought that young Francis might challenge his record, which is why he gave him every opportunity to succeed. The kid yearned for success, so why not give him a chance to earn it? Losing Francis hurt, but his death and failure to apprehend the Mutie scum was unacceptable. Someone had to provide DeSouza with some answers, and John Harris was on the hook.

DeSouza heard a faint knock on his door. "Enter," he barked.

John Harris poked his head through the door and asked, "You wanted to see me, sir?"

"What do I always tell my officers about leading with their heads? C'mon in, John, and have a seat. I want to talk about your report."

John entered the director's office. The office had the cold, sterile feel of most of the new buildings in Cincuenta Yuno. The walls were white. The furniture was gray and black. Everything in the office had sharp angles: the director's desk, his chairs for guests, a corner table for less formal conversations, the picture frames that contained inspirational quotes, and the windows with horizontal blinds.

John walked timidly towards the angular black chair. It looked cold and uncomfortable. Nothing about the director's office was welcoming.

"Sit down, John. You're not in any trouble, so spare me the tail-between-the-legs routine."

John sat down.

"I wanted to give you my condolences, John. I know losing a partner is always tough. I want you to know I'm here for you if you need to talk about it. If you're not comfortable talking to me, I can find you someone to talk to."

"No sir, it's fine — I mean, it's not fine, but I'm dealing with it."

"I just wanted to get some clarity around your report."

"What did you want to know, sir?" John said, unable to shake his timid tone. He knew he was in dangerous territory.

"Well, I've been going over and over the report. I can't quite understand how this female Mutie, who, according to your description, couldn't be more than 115 pounds, could kill Francis and escape?"

DeSouza was on the hunt. He knew the game was afoot and was not to be denied. The prize was the truth because he knew it wasn't within the pages of John's report. DeSouza watched John squirm after being asked the question.

"Uh — what do you mean, sir?"

"Well, I can't understand how I have a dead officer on my hands, and all I have is this report with barely any details. Baisley was younger, stronger, and more driven than you, so why are you sitting in front of me instead of him? From where I'm sitting, I should be discussing this with Baisley, not you. Did you hesitate when you saw the Mutant?"

John's jaw clenched. DeSouza's remarks were precisely why John was sitting in front of DeSouza instead of Baisley.

"Well?" DeSouza prodded, trying to get a response from John. The meeting had ceased being an employer/employee interaction and had become an interrogation. John knew as much and wondered how long he could hold out.

"Officer Harris, are you going to just sit there, or are you going to answer me?" DeSouza barked. "This report is only good for wiping my ass!"

"You're right!" John finally relented.

"Right about what, Officer Harris?"

"Francis was younger, stronger, and more driven than me, but that's why he's dead!"

"I'm sorry. I'm having some trouble understanding your logic, Officer Harris."

"We were on a stakeout, and that brat went solo on me, trying to be the hero and grab the glory."

"I don't understand, Officer Harris. How could that be if you were on a stakeout together? Did you desert your post? Is that why you're peddling this crap?"

"No, sir! I was asleep," John said, his voice dripping with regret, his brow gleaming with beads of sweat.

DeSouza perked up. "What was that, Officer Harris? You were asleep?" DeSouza leaned back in his chair, the tone of his voice softening. He had captured his prize.

"Sir, we were the only ones working in that district. You had us there round the clock. Sir, you remember how it is in the field, don't you?"

"You'll have to refresh my memory, John."

"Well, we took watch shifts, and during Francis' shift, the Mutie appeared. I guess he wanted to be the hero, so he didn't wake me. That little prick didn't trust me anyway. Sir, I've been on the force for a long time, and I may not be the next in line for Sergeant, but I've been here for a long time because I know what it takes to get the job done."

"I know, John. You're one of my finest beat officers, which is why I partnered Baisley with you."

John sighed. His body relaxed. He didn't feel like a cornered animal anymore.

"Anyway, I woke up to a large explosion, it sounded like a gun firing, so I was on full alert. I found the Mutie standing over Francis. It was hard to tell what was going on, but I knew something was wrong. I *did* apprehend the Mutie. She was in my grasp, but I was careless. I thought the Mutie was the only one there, but that Mule must've been helping her. I've been looking at Mule files all day trying to find her. She took me by surprise and attacked me — tased me, the scum. They both escaped. Francis is dead, and there's nothing to show for it." John's lip began to quiver from the emotion. John wasn't cocky, but he knew that he wasn't a liability to his partners or the department. Francis' death had him questioning that.

"John, it's always tough losing a partner, especially the way it went down. Here's what's going to happen. First, I want you to give me an updated account of the events. But more importantly, I want you to lead the operation to capture the perps."

"Me, Sir? I've never run an op before. I never really wanted — "

"Listen, I know it isn't your strength, but you know the streets better than most beat officers in Cincuenta Yuno. You've had a close look at both the perps and... I'm offering you some redemption."

"But sir, you have the sketches from my description — the city maps are all digitized, and I've never led an op before."

"I know, John, but you know what *doesn't* appear on the maps? Your memory. The Department has sketches, but I'm sure you'd recognize those two by sight. No sketch is going to give an officer that reaction time. Lastly, I'm giving this to you because you need this. I know this will eat you up; I've seen it happen to other officers. Not many people get a shot at redemption, John. Take it."

"I'll do it, sir," John said with conviction. Something about DeSouza's words lit a fire in him. Something he hadn't felt in a long time.

"Good. Now, get that new report to me before you leave — and I want a printout of the Mule district letting me know where you think the hot spots might be. In the meantime, find me that damn Mule from the profiles."

"Yes, sir!"

"We'll meet back at twenty-two hundred to review and discuss our next steps."

"Yes, sir!" John Harris barked, leaping to his feet. His uniform creaked under the quick movement. John marched out of the Director's office brimming with confidence and purpose.

DeSouza smiled as he watched Officer Harris leave. DeSouza liked John despite his complacency. He knew what he was going to get out of Officer Harris. He was predictable and dependable and didn't leave DeSouza worrying about surprises. DeSouza believed John when he said that Officer Baisley's death resulted from his unnecessary risk.

Risk was foreign to Officer Harris' character, making his report so suspicious. Officer Harris would never have participated in such stupidity. He would have called for backup. He was forced into a situation that was entirely foreign to him, which is why he failed. DeSouza expected as much from Officer Baisley. Risk can go two ways; you win, or you lose. Francis lost, and the cost was his life. If he had won, it would've meant a promotion and DeSouza checking over his shoulder earlier than expected.

DeSouza didn't mind the competition for his job. Many people were chasing his position. It kept him on his toes. He knew the department lost a great officer with Francis Baisley's death. He also knew it would plague Officer Harris. Francis would be missed, but DeSouza couldn't let that cost him two officers, especially since Officer Harris didn't have the greatest reputation in the department.

The department encouraged high performance. Officer Harris was content to just perform. If Harris didn't do something to redeem himself, DeSouza would be hard-pressed to find him another willing partner. With ridicule and a partner's death following him throughout the department, DeSouza was afraid he would inevitably lose Harris.

DeSouza needed Officer Harris to work harder than ever to shed his peers' skepticism. After all, DeSouza needed officers like John Harris; he needed reliable achievers who had no desire to be the department's head. The department couldn't run with a bunch of leaders. It needed some followers. Officer Harris fit that bill perfectly.

DeSouza rose to his feet and walked over to a tall window overlooking Cincuenta Yuno. He opened the blinds to reveal the setting sun. The fading light stained Director DeSouza's office a brilliant orange. He squinted to survey his domain, wanting desperately to know what the Mutie and Mule slime were up to. DeSouza had no desire to have a Mutant infiltration attached to his legacy. The time was eighteen hundred hours; Officer Harris had four hours to prove himself. DeSouza wasn't sure he'd deliver, but he had to put some trust in Officer Harris if he was going to pull it off.

DeSouza sat back in his chair and reclined, letting the filtered warmth of the remaining rays sink in. This was a common ritual when he needed to think and find some peace amidst the chaos. He cleared his mind and allowed the numerous paths and possibilities to reveal themselves. This is what DeSouza did best — it was how he anticipated the Mutie infiltration in the first place. He was right and almost had them. Now he was going to ensure that Officer Harris would catch these two and rid the city of the vermin.

***

Director Franco DeSouza watched night fall over Cincuenta Yuno. Twenty-two hundred hours was approaching quickly. DeSouza had begun fighting his doubt about thirty minutes prior. He looked at the large, cold tombstones that rose from the desert. Society's shining achievement. They had vanquished their greatest foe: a failing environment. The buildings were pitch-black. They looked deserted, like the ruins of the old urban centers of the Americas. DeSouza read about a time when buildings remained lit throughout the night because it was cheaper to do so. Now, buildings were only lit when required. Conserving precious energy was integral in this new era.

DeSouza lived for his moments of solitude. He couldn't imagine what life was like when people were perpetually connected. He took a deep breath and enjoyed it being the only sound to fill his office. During the day, he never got a moment's rest. Usually, his evenings consisted of reviewing paperwork from home and taking calls from his on-shift supervisors for assistance. DeSouza couldn't help being a workaholic, but the nature of his job meant he had to be. He hated leaving things unfinished anyway. There was always more work to do. DeSouza tried to keep his docket clear. Work unfinished would plague his thoughts. He knew that from many sleepless nights. He needed closure. It's that attitude that usually condemns one to solitude and loneliness. Who would be a partner to someone who'd always have to place work ahead of everything? Always being second place to a first love that only demanded more without giving anything in return.

DeSouza did have a partner once. That was long ago. His wife, Donna, used to stay up late with him. She liked working through his cases with him. She was so clever. Her big, hazel eyes caught every detail. Words on reports told her the secrets and details that the writers hadn't intended. DeSouza owed a lot of his success to her. Her ability to recognize flaws in reports, evidence, and testimonies made his career — she knew how to ask the right questions, and DeSouza was great at getting answers. They were a perfect team, and DeSouza often spent his time alone thinking about her and the child he never knew.

DeSouza remembered the day his wife told him the news. It was a joyous day. They spent an entire evening lost in each other's company, discussing the future: names, the nursery, education, and jobs. The future couldn't have looked brighter then…

CHAPTER 4

Helia's eyes darted around the scribbled markings on the floor of Ari's apartment. Ari easily carved out the extensive sewage system she had known as a second home. The linoleum didn't stand a chance against the pressure Ari applied with her strong hand. Her knife was dull, but it didn't make a difference. She quickly and effortlessly fashioned a crude reproduction of the sewage system for Helia's review.

Helia admired Ari's ability and agility. Her first impression was off — Ari was beginning to pleasantly surprise her. She was obviously quite strong. Helia noticed the muscle definition in Ari's arms as she carved the maps, vandalizing her floor. Ari's willingness to deface her home showed an ability to improvise. No pencil, no paper, no problem. The map also told Helia that Ari could take in mass amounts of information and reproduce it quite effectively. As Helia studied the carvings, she digested the information. A lot of nuances were missing from the maps she had studied in the Freelands.

She peppered Ari with questions as she worked.

"So, this connects multiple passages?"

"Are all these passages the same distance underground?"

"Where does this passage lead to?"

After reviewing the maps and receiving answers that met her needs, Helia leaned back and closed her eyes. Ari watched her soft features relax as her eyes darted beneath her lids. She couldn't believe that Helia had recovered entirely. She looked flawless. Ari had no idea how beautiful Helia was when she first laid eyes on her. She was battered to a pulp — swollen and bruised. But now, she was sleek, and her body strong with sinewy muscles. Ari watched Helia in her meditative state. Helia opened her eyes suddenly and looked at Ari. Ari jumped and quickly looked away, beginning to color. Helia smiled, knowing that Ari was watching her.

"I've got it. I have your maps committed to memory."

Ari, grateful that Helia had pretended not to notice her staring, replied, "Great, we leave tomorrow after I've done some preliminary scouting."

Helia suddenly sat very erect. Her eyes widened as she looked into nothingness.

"Wha — " Ari began to ask.

"*Shhh.*"

***

Officers Sheik and Reid were sitting in their Department of Sanitation vehicle when they received the call. It had been a slow day. They had cruised their district, noticing nothing interesting. The Mules in their region were all working without disruption. They hadn't seen any strange faces, but they were on high alert, having heard the rumors that a Mutie had infiltrated Cincuenta Yuno. They had just finished talking about what they would do if they saw the Mutie on their beat. Long-winded stories all ended the same way: medals of commendation and promotions. Neither of the officers had seen a Mutant before, so they began listing ways they would be able to recognize one.

"Green skin."

"Horns."

"A tail."

Officer Sheik had been in the Department only a short time. As with most officers, he had high aspirations of becoming a unit leader within five years. Sheik was just twenty-two years old. He was the perfect physical specimen. His smooth, brown complexion and chiseled features made him popular with most people he encountered. He had absolute confidence that he would achieve his goals.

Officer Sheik watched the street with his dark eyes. They caught every detail. He watched people's interactions on the sparsely populated street. Sheik was on the hunt for anything suspicious. Sheik and Reid hadn't spoken a word for almost two hours. It wasn't that the partners did not get along, but they were competitive. Officer Reid was only one year older than Officer Sheik and had his eyes on a promotion, too. They sat in silence, hoping to be the first one to spot the Mutant.

The partners had agreed that whoever spotted the Mutie would get credit for the collar while the other would profess to only assisting the arrest. The two agreed that this would be the best course of action. Better for one to get ahead than for both to stagnate in Cincuenta Yuno, waiting into their mid-thirties to move up the ladder.

Officer Reid looked just as intently as his partner at the street before them. His icy blue eyes coolly surveyed the street. Reid stole glances at Officer Sheik. He strained to discern if his partner saw anything he might have missed. Reid's biggest fear was losing the competition that the two partners were engaged in. Pride ran thick through each of their veins. Reid was older. To him, a year was a lifetime of knowledge and experience that Sheik couldn't hope to understand. If he lost to Sheik, practically a baby, he could be taking orders from him. Reid would rather quit the department than stomach that from someone obviously his junior.

"Officers Reid and Sheik, come in…" their car radio crackled.

Reid quickly took the CB and glared at Sheik, relishing his victory.

"Officer Reid here… and Sheik. What have you got for us?"

Sheik sneered at Reid for the way he responded to the call.

"We have a code 121 yellow in the Mule district on 12 Gore Avenue, Unit 714. Please investigate. Suspects are considered highly dangerous, so be on guard. They are to be brought in for questioning, so do not use lethal force!"

"Got it, we're on our way, and we'll bring 'em in by end of shift," Reid replied, winking at his partner.

"You bastard," Sheik snapped. "Why do you always have to make it seem like you're in charge? It makes me sound incompetent to the CO."

"C'mon, Sheik. Y'know, I'm just doing it to push your buttons. It looks like our little bet is off. We'll have to collar these fugitives together."

"Deal. Let's peel out!"

Reid's hands darted quickly to prevent Sheik from activating the siren.

"Let's go in silent. The siren may tip 'em off. Don't worry about getting there. This baby's got tons of power, and I'll get us through the traffic easily enough."

Sheik nodded in agreement. "Cherries, though?"

Reid nodded.

The partners knew that they played off each other's strengths. Neither looked forward to leaving the other behind when they were promoted. The lights flashed. Reid slammed the vehicle into gear, and they were off.

***

Officers Reid and Sheik arrived at the building. Reid turned off the vehicle's engine. He looked at Sheik and said, "Alright, they're on the seventh floor. The unit is on the northwest corner of the building, number 714. Do we want to split up to cover all exits or storm the place?"

Sheik contemplated the options.

"Let's look at the specs to see how many possible escape routes there are."

"On-screen," Officer Reid barked to the LCD tilted in his direction. The screen flickered and lit up, glowing in front of him.

"Floor plans to 12 Gore Ave."

The floor plans appeared.

"Seventh floor."

Reid tilted the screen in Sheik's direction. Their eyes darted, studying the layout of the building. Sheik was the first to break the silence.

"Okay, other than the entrance, it looks like the only other exit point is a fire escape."

"Alright, let's check the fire escape. It might actually be a better point of entry," Reid recommended.

Sheik nodded. They both got out of their vehicle and walked toward the building. Slowly edging along the southern wall, they worked their way westward and peered around the corner of the building. The fire escape was horribly dilapidated and rusted. It couldn't hold the weight of a child. They both resumed their position against the south wall.

"Well, it doesn't look like anyone could get down that without plummeting to their death," Reid remarked.

Sheik nodded. "Let's storm the building. They can't go anywhere without breaking something. If they jump, they won't be getting far."

They both entered the building from the front, walking stealthily through the apartment building lobby. They were in stark contrast to the dilapidated building. Two brand-new officers in glistening black polycarbonate armor. The entrance had marble walls and pillars that were cracked and crumbling, revealing their rusted wire skeletons. The floor was a brownish orange carpeting interwoven with a series of white diamonds covered with stains. The two officers reached a stairwell that had no door. They entered one after the other, alternating the responsibility of checking whether there was any danger ahead.

Slowly working their way up the stairwell, the two officers held their breath, trying to avoid the stench. The railings were topped with orange plastic that bubbled and peeled from years of moisture, revealing a naked rusted rail where the orange plastic was no more. The walls were off-white. It was difficult to discern if they were once white but had yellowed over time or if it was the intended hue. Chunks of plaster were missing, revealing the gray concrete beneath. The linoleum beneath their feet was sticky.

The officers reached the seventh floor. Reid turned to Sheik.

"Alright, power up." They each turned on their tasers, which let out high-pitched squeals. "You ready?" Reid asked. His eyes were electric, charged like their tasers.

"You know it," Sheik responded, revealing a quiver in his voice that Reid couldn't place. Was it excitement or fear?

"Alright, I'll take first. Check if the hall is cleared."

Sheik obeyed, confirming the hallway was safe.

"Check."

On Sheik's word, Reid burst into the seventh-floor hallway. Inching closer to apartment 714, the two paused at their destination, standing in front of the browned door. It had a speckled brass seven and a four with a missing number between them. The officers looked at each other.

"This is it," Reid confirmed, looking at his partner.

Sheik looked back at the hallway. The peeling, dingy wallpaper was brushed with a faded gold design. The stained, rusty-orange diamond carpeted floor matched the lobby. Sheik looked at his partner.

"Yep, this is it."

"On three, I'm kicking down the door. On your all-clear, I'll burst in. Got it?"

"Yep."

"Alright then, on three. One, two, three!"

***

"What's wrong?" Ari asked Helia.

"We have to leave."

"What? You were practically beaten to death earlier today! How can we — "

"We have no time! They're here already!"

"Who?"

"They. We need to move, and we can't go out the front. Is there any other way out of here?"

"Well, there's a fire escape, but — "

"Good, take me to it."

"I don't — "

"No arguing! Take me to it now!" Helia demanded. She knew that danger was near. She could smell the pheromones in the air. There were two distinct scents, and they were aggressive. They were getting ready to pounce. Ari shrank away from Helia's snap. Helia noticed the wince. She felt bad, but she was a soldier. It was time to act. She knew their lives were in danger, and there was no time to act any other way. It was time to move.

Ari rose to her feet and mumbled, "Follow me," in a defeated tone. Helia leaped to her feet.

She pulled off her dress as she rose. "Phew! Glad to get out of that costume."

Helia stood in a black battle suit. It was lightly armored. Polycarbonate plates were placed throughout the suit to not inhibit movement but still provide protection. Her zip gun and hunting knife were strapped to hips. Ari paused, admiring Helia's warrior physique. She colored and led the way in silence.

Helia looked at Ari sympathetically. *Poor Ari — she has no idea what kind of danger she's in*, Helia thought to herself.

Ari took her to a window and pointed. "There it is," she grunted.

Helia looked down at the rusted, decrepit relic that pretended to provide some measure of safety.

"It won't hold either of us," Helia mumbled to herself.

She could tell that the fire escape supports would snap under *any* weight. There was another building across the street, but it was too far to jump. Helia might be able to make it and possibly scale the wall, but there was no way she could take Ari with her. Ari couldn't follow her, nor could Helia carry Ari's weight and hope to be as agile. Helia looked at the fire escape again. An idea popped into her mind.

"Ari — quickly, I need you on the fire escape."

"Are you crazy? I'm not getting on that thing! It'll be the last thing I do!"

"There's no time. Get out there now!" Helia yelled.

"I said *no*! I'm not going to — "

CRASH!

The door was shattered, and with one quick leap, Ari was on the fire escape. She heard it creak under her weight. The rusted structure feebly tried to do its job. Ari heard a whizzing noise over her head. They must be shooting at her.

Oh no, Helia! Ari thought to herself. Ari looked up to see Helia's body grab hold of the outside railing of the fire escape. It wasn't shooting. Helia had whizzed by Ari's head, her black outline moving like a shadow. She was on the outside of the railing. Ari moved to grab her, afraid that she'd plummet to her death.

"Stay where you are and hold on as tight as you can!" Helia yelled frantically. Ari froze and held on to the stairs of the fire escape.

SNAP, SNAP, SNAP!

The brackets that held the fire escape to the wall were breaking off. Ari looked back at Helia, her heart racing.

"We're gonna fall!" she warned.

"I know. Hold on."

The fire escape gave way with a loud groan. Helia leaped from the window, grabbed the outside railing, and yanked the ancient structure hard enough to free it from the wall. She was now under the rusted relic as it fell away from the building. Helia guided their fall toward the neighboring structure, which brought their descent to an abrupt halt.

CLANG!

They stopped falling. Ari could feel the vibrations of the fire escape resonate throughout her body. Helia released her grasp from the twisted railing and dropped delicately to the pavement beneath her. They were now less than a story above the ground.

"Come on, Ari, move! They've spotted us!"

Ari looked up to see two heads poking out of her window. She dropped to the ground, landing on her back with a resounding thud.

"Are you okay?" Helia asked.

Ari sprung to her feet. "I'm fine! Let's move to the sewers — we'll be safe there."

"Lead the way!"

"I thought you had an id-eh-ctick memory!" Ari smiled, grabbing Helia's arm to lead her to the sewer entrance.

"It's eidetic, and yes, you're right, but you showed me the sewage system, not how to get there. Once I'm down there, no problem," Helia huffed as they both ran toward safety.

"Oh, *I see.* Stop here." Ari bent over to lift the sewer lid. "Here we are," she said in a straining voice, revealing a black pit. Helia could hear running water below — from her estimate, it was about a twenty-foot drop.

"The ladder to get down is over — " It was too late; Ari's direction was cut short. Helia leaped into the pit. Ari shook her head as she began to climb down, sliding the sewer lid back over her as they descended into safety.

***

CRASH!

"Check!" Sheik yelled.

Officer Reid bounded into the apartment, followed by Officer Sheik. Reid whirled around to find himself alone in the room with his partner. A flash of color caught the corner of his eye.

"That room!" Reid yelled, pointing deeper into the apartment.

They moved quickly toward the movement but stopped abruptly, only to find a dead end. Noticing a mirror on the wall, Reid cursed himself. *It* was the source of the movement.

"Damn it!"

"What is it?" Sheik asked. "Where are they? Do you see them?"

Reid looked in the mirror. Another flash of movement. Turning around, he noticed the kitchen window.

"There!" Reid yelled, pointing to the kitchen.

Sheik turned around to see an empty kitchen. Sheik was about to open his mouth to question his partner when his train of thought was interrupted.

SNAP, SNAP, SNAP!

As they approached the kitchen, they could hear yelling.

"We're gonna fall!" a raspy female voice yelled.

"I know! Hold on," another female voice replied.

Then they heard a loud metallic groan.

CLANG!

They popped their heads out the window.

Below they could see a stocky Mule jump to her feet and grab a woman's arm. They both began to run.

"Damn!" Reid yelled. "Track where they're going."

"Got it," Sheik responded. No time to question Reid under the current circumstances. He knew his partner was upset. Reid's misjudgment may have let the fugitives get away. Reid pulled his head in as Sheik watched the two targets run until they disappeared. Sheik left the window when they were out of sight and walked through the worn apartment. Drawers, pillows, and furniture were strewn about. Reid had pulled out everything looking for evidence to bring back to the central office.

"You find anything?" Sheik asked when he joined Reid in the main room.

"Nothing, this place is barren," Reid responded dejectedly.

"Well, gather what we can, and let's head out," Sheik said in a consoling tone.

"Is pursuit possible?" Reid asked.

"No, they're long gone."

Reid's shoulders slumped. "Let's close up shop here, grab some clothes, anything we can find. Maybe we can run a DNA test on the stuff they left behind. Let's give CO as much as we can."

"Got it."

They both continued in silence, gathering all that they could. The partners felt the failure of the day. They avoided each other's eyes as they worked, finishing in disappointment.

"Leave a drone behind," Reid said with a tone of finality. "We're through here."

Sheik unpacked the metallic sentry. He pressed a button at the top of the disk-like entity, which vibrated as a series of multicolored lights danced as it booted up. "Done," Sheik informed his partner.

"Good, let's move out then."

They left the apartment to the robotic guard. They closed the door behind them, taking everything they could find, they left the apartment, mistaking Ari's map on the floor for some sort of Mule artwork.

***

Bap Bap.

The rapping at the door woke Director DeSouza from his trance. He whirled around to check the time. It was twenty-two hundred hours.

Officer Harris' voice penetrated the director's door. "Ah, sir, I have the information you wanted."

"Come in, Harris. Let's see what you've got."

Harris entered the room cautiously with a tablet in hand.

"Sir, where do you want me to hook this up?"

"Sit down at my desk, John. There's a free port here; I'll sit up front so you can lead me through what you have."

Officer Harris moved behind the director's desk, feeling horribly uncomfortable. DeSouza sat in one of the guest chairs, adjusting to get the best view.

John booted up the tablet. He took a seat in the director's chair and winced as it creaked under his unfamiliar body. DeSouza noticed his discomfort.

"Don't worry, Harris." DeSouza smiled, trying to put Harris at ease.

"I — just feels weird, sittin' on this side of the desk, sir."

"Don't be so modest. It suits you," DeSouza lied. "Now, let's see what you've got."

The projector kicked in, and Officer Harris loaded up the first file. The wall flickered with a collage of light that struggled to form a fuzzy image. Officer Harris manipulated the projection lens. The picture came into focus, revealing a grizzly-faced woman looking very displeased.

"Who am I looking at?" DeSouza asked.

"This is Mule 016257, given name: Arianwyn. She's a sewer rat, sir, responsible for taking samples and general cleaning duties throughout the sewage systems of Cincuenta Yuno."

"Do we have any information on this Mule? Is she a conspirator with any known Mutie organizations?"

"No, sir. Her actions have been monitored sporadically. She's been red-flagged due to inconsistent work attendance, but the Mule case workers discovered she has a pretty strong addiction to alcohol."

"Well, why are you showing her to me, Officer Harris?"

"This is the Mule who prevented me from bringing in the Mutie, sir. She was the one who attacked me."

"What is her involvement then, Harris? If she isn't a conspirator, then why would she risk her life to save a Mutie? Did we get any intel from Hector about this Mule or any other Mules before he expired?"

Harris shook his head. "Nothing in the interrogation transcript, sir." He paused.

"What is it, Harris? You have to let me know what you're thinking."

"Sir, I'm not sure she knew it *was* a Mutie. For all I know, she just happened upon the scene or something. She may have been drunk and up for a fight. There's a lot of that on her profile."

"Still, once a Mule is black-flagged for transgressions that deem them unfit for work, they're destroyed. Why would she get involved? Does our intelligence indicate where she was known to frequent?"

"Yes, sir. She was a frequent patron of Helena's Tavern."

"So she was a patron of a conspirator's bar and saved a Mutie who entered Cincuenta Yuno through the sewers. Something tells me that Mule is more connected than we're giving her credit. Notify the central Mule processing division and have some agents review this Mule's file more closely. See if we can come up with anything. Let's send someone to collar her and bring her in. Maybe we'll find the Mutie at the same time."

"Already ordered, sir. A unit was dispatched to the Mule's living quarters. Reid and Sheik reported back. The Mule's unit was recently vacated. There were two inhabitants. Our records show that the unit is a single-person dwelling."

"Do you think she was housing the Mutie?"

"It seems she may have brought her there after attacking me, sir. The officers collected evidence to run DNA, but I don't think the results will tell us anything we don't already know."

"Alright, what else do you have?"

"Well, working under the hypothesis that the Mutie was set to rendezvous with the owner of Helena's tavern, we have to assume that she'll return to the location to try and obtain any information that may have been left behind."

"Good — have you blocked off all the possible entry points?"

"Sir, that brings me to my other file."

Officer Harris switched files on the slate. The wall flickered and revealed a map.

"This, sir, is the city's sewage structure. As you can see, directly under Helena's Tavern is a hub. There are several possible entry points into the Tavern via the sewage ducts. It's sandwiched between two larger structures, which would enable it to be penetrated from within, and there are four possible street access points."

"Good job, Harris. If the Mule isn't in her dwelling, it's likely that they are already en route to Helena's Tavern."

"Right, sir! Several drones have been deployed to cover the access points, but as you know, they are useless in the sewage structures. I'm requesting a full complement of officers for ground and sewer support."

"I agree. Let's get a team together and see if we can apprehend the two fugitives."

"Sir, I'm requesting that we have some heavy artillery deployed. This Mutie killed Officer Baisley with her bare hands. No tasers or rubber bullets this time out. Let's learn from our mistakes."

"Harris, I want the Mutie alive."

"Why, sir? If we exterminate the Mutie, don't we exterminate the threat?"

"Only for today. I want to get the source. That's really the only way to exterminate the threat."

Well, sir, let's get some sharpshooters in then. The Mule doesn't matter though, does she, sir?"

"I want her alive, too. I don't think our intelligence is up to speed on Mule activities. She may have information on other conspirators. I like the strategy. I'm putting you on point, Harris. I'll get on the horn and get the units deployed. I want you on-site to receive all officers; there's no time for a formal debrief. We need to move on this now!"

"Yes, sir!"

"Now get suited up and move! I'll mobilize the units. Expect to receive them shortly after you arrive on-site."

"Yes, sir!" John disconnected the tablet and prepared his exit.

"Leave it, Harris, just get moving," DeSouza barked.

Officer Harris stood up stiffly. "Yes, sir!"

Harris marched out of the room in boot camp fashion, not wanting to raise the director's ire again.

DeSouza moved behind his desk. He looked at the map projected on his wall. That bastard Hector had the perfect location. It was a strategic gem. From there, anyone could lay siege to the city from underground. It was sheer luck they brought him in when they did. Who knows what might have happened otherwise?

DeSouza focused on the sewage hub. He visually traced all the outflowing points to key places in the city — it was like a series of veins under the skin of the Cincuenta Yuno. One of the arteries was right under the Department of Sanitation building. DeSouza's eyes caught some disparities in the map. There were a number of dead ends and locations that didn't look familiar to him, and DeSouza knew Cincuenta Yuno inside and out. His ignorance sat like a ball in the pit of his stomach. It was his neglect that had resulted in the current situation. He was staring directly into his failures.

DeSouza pounded his desk, violently shoving his thumb on his conference bridge.

"Hello… Sir? Sir, Officer Tatum here. What can I do for you?" a crackling voice inquired.

"Tatum, we have a serious breach in Cincuenta Yuno. I need your boys brought in and deployed, fully armed and armored, in the Mule district on the double."

"Sir? A breach? But how?"

"No time for questions, Tatum!" the director yelled. "Just do it! Officer Harris will rendezvous with you at the hotspot we took down the other day. He will get you up to speed."

"Officer Harris, Sir? But — "

"What did I say about questions, Tatum? You have trouble hearing me? Am I breaking up or something? Harris is on point for this one. You take all orders from him. *Is that clear?*" DeSouza yelled.

"Yes, sir," Tatum replied, his wounded pride ringing across the crackling reception.

"Good! We have a Mutie on the inside. One officer is already dead. We need to take her out now!"

"Understood, sir. My team will be assembled and deployed immediately. ETA is fifteen minutes."

"You've got five."

"Yes, Sir!"

DeSouza released the button on the conference bridge. He looked at the remaining buttons labeled with his unit leaders' names. Tatum down, four to go. DeSouza decided to pull some tight security around Cincuenta Yuno. Nothing in and nothing out. He was going to use all his units to make sure that the issue was contained and resolved. He looked at the next leader; DeSouza didn't enjoy having to lay it on his leadership team. It wasn't their fault. It was his and his short-sightedness, but he needed them to move, and if he had to be a jerk to light a fire under them, then that's what he would do. DeSouza violently thumbed the next button in sequence.

"Hello… Sir? Sir, Officer Adabie here. What can I do for you?" a confused voice crackled back at him.

CHAPTER 5

The rush of chunky sewage over her ankles made Helia quiver in disgust. She looked up, holding her breath, to see what was taking Ari so long. Helia was in complete darkness. She waited for her night vision to adjust to her new setting. Helia's pupils began to dilate, exposing the rods and cones of her retinas. She began to make out shapes and walls. She looked up the ladder and saw Ari's wide frame slowly creeping down the rungs.

Ari made a splash as she hit the bottom. Helia nudged her. "What took you so long?" she inquired, somewhat playfully.

With her inquiry, Helia took a full breath of the sewer's foul air. The stench assaulted her faculties, making her stagger. The sewer walls spun like the liquid between her feet. Ari's concerned face seemed to stretch. She knew Helia was about to faint. Ari quickly grabbed her to keep Helia from falling.

"Hold on. You're gonna be alright. Most people have trouble breathing down here." Helia regained her balance, and the walls stopped swimming with the help of Ari's firm grip.

"They have these at all the entrance points," Ari said, reaching toward a wall-mounted compartment. She took out a mask and passed it to Helia. Still queasy, Helia slid the mask in place. As she took deep breaths, her eyes regained focus. Ari reached back into the compartment and produced an LED torch. Helia began to motion for Ari to stop, but it was too late. Ari lit the handheld lantern. The light flowed into Helia's fully dilated pupils. She screamed in pain, hunched over, and covered her eyes. Her rods and cones felt like they had retreated into her brain.

"Are you okay? Are you going to be sick? Is the mask not working? Take it off if you're gonna be sick, okay?" Ari said in a concerned and soothing voice as she rubbed Helia's back.

Helia recovered from the short-term pain. Her eyes adjusted to the new light that flooded the cavernous sewers of Cincuenta Yuno. Helia didn't have the heart to yell at Ari again. She knew Ari was just trying to be helpful, and Ari wouldn't have been able to see without the light.

"That's pretty bright! Next time warn me so I can cover my eyes or something," Helia said, trying her best to sound playful and not scornful.

"Oh yeah, sorry, didn't think of that. I don't usually have anyone else to think about down here," Ari said bashfully, hoping she hadn't done any harm. "I guess we'd better get moving. If they knew to come to my place to try and find you, they probably know we went into the sewers."

"It looks like we're breaking into Helena's Tavern sooner rather than later," Helia stated in a matter-of-fact tone.

"What, are you crazy? We should lie low for a while," Ari replied, shocked at Helia's train of thought.

"No. We have to strike now before the Department of Sanitation has time to prepare for us."

"What if they already are?"

"We'll have to take that chance."

"If we hide out, they may have to broaden their search. We could strike then."

"I don't think so, Ari. I'm a Freeborn infiltrator. They won't rest until I'm apprehended. Their resources far surpass the two of us. Our best opportunity is to strike while they're still mobilizing. Every moment we wait, we're ruining our chances at success."

"It's suicide."

"You keep saying that. Don't worry. I'll keep you safe."

"Hey, let's remember who saved who here," Ari responded, a little injured that Helia thought *she* needed protection.

"That's right, and I just repaid you back there. We're even. Next time, you owe me," Helia said with a twinkle in her eyes reflecting the LED lamp. Helia was doing her best to deflect Ari's concern. She needed Ari on her side. Ari smiled and relented.

"Alright, let's move. It's this way," Ari directed.

"I know," Helia responded.

"Oh yeah, I forgot, ick-ah-deck-tick memory."

"Eidetic. You're doing that on purpose now."

The two began to make their way toward Helena's Tavern through the sewers.

***

Officer Harris overlooked the chaotic scene he was in command of. Drones whizzed by his head as officers ran to get into position. Harris barked orders to the officers.

"I want every exit covered. As soon as the alarms are tripped, we move in. I don't want anyone playing hero. Only proceed on my mark. Thomas, back up Henderson. Wang, we need you on the roof."

Harris felt in control. He was surprised at how comfortable he was leading an operation. Harris initially doubted Director DeSouza's judgment to have him on point. Since he received his assignment, he couldn't stop sweating. Harris had been riding a wave of nausea that swelled every time he thought of failing the director. Failure was John Harris' biggest fear. He was much more comfortable in situations he considered safe. Trying new things, especially when so much was at stake, scared him.

Regardless, John Harris was not a quitter. He prided himself on being reliable, someone his director and peers could count on. He put them first, which is how he found himself in his current predicament. But to his surprise, his confidence grew with every order. His fear of failure became a strength. It gave him an unexpected insight that enabled him to see numerous variables. He had officers on the roof with a pre-cut square ready to plunge through on his command. Drones were placed at the team's rear to ensure that nothing would sneak up behind them. They could also act as a second line of defense if the fugitives somehow broke through. Heat sensors were placed inside Helena's Tavern. As soon as a warm body entered, Harris would know about it. He also planted officers at all sewer access points in case the fugitives decided to retreat. Once deployed, they would press toward the central hub of the sewer and the entrance to Helena's Tavern. They would pressure the fugitives from all sides. Harris waited patiently. He didn't want to jeopardize his officers or risk blowing the operation with overzealousness. John Harris had constructed a well-laid trap. He was ready for the fugitives and prepared to snap down on them as soon as they took the bait.

"Liu, I want you to enter from the east side, not the west. Join Nanjad's unit. Move it!" Harris activated his Polycom. The voice unit would keep channels of communication open to all his officers. Integrated with an officer's armor, the invisible device enabled two-way voice transmission in the assault units' helmets. "Green unit, are you in position?"

"Yes sir, waiting for your mark." A crackling voice responded.

"Orange unit, status?"

"We're in position, sir, awaiting orders."

Sir, Harris thought to himself. He could get used to that.

Officer Harris often thought that he knew better than most of his peers. He had walked the same streets, keeping order, longer than anyone in his division. Most of them used Harris' division as a stepping stone for their careers. Harris was a rare officer. He was satisfied in his station and had no desire to move elsewhere in the Department of Sanitation. He thought it was fitting that he was now being called "Sir" by those who used to look at him and his inertia with disdain. The fear he once had melted away as the minutes of the evening passed. As dawn approached, Harris felt that he was advancing to a new era in his life. This was something he could get used to. As he barked orders and watched subordinates scatter to fulfill his strategy, Harris realized something. This felt right.

WHOOP, WHOOP, WHOOP!

***

Ari and Helia waded towards their destination when Ari stopped and looked upward. Helia paused, matching her partner. After studying Ari for clues, Helia asked, "What are you stopping for? This isn't it. According to your map, the entrance to Helena's Tavern should be further down."

"You're right. Good memory, but I'm wondering whether it would be best to get onto the street first or directly enter Helena's Tavern," Ari cautioned.

"Let's get in and out. The fastest way to do that is to strike at the center and move out," Helia stated with conviction.

Uncertain of the strategy, Ari responded, "But if it's a trap, we run the risk of being captured and killed."

"That's the risk no matter what we do. Anyway we look at it, I'm prepared for a fight. I think it's best to strike closest to our target and retreat."

"Maybe you're right. I don't know what the point of being cautious is now. I guess I threw that away a long time ago." Ari tailed off, almost mumbling the last words to herself.

"Good. Since we're in agreement, let's keep moving. Time wasted is spent by the enemy; we're giving them time to get ready for us," Helia preached, kicking herself for sounding too much like Troy. She didn't like it when he said those platitudes. She liked herself less for sounding like him.

"Alright, we're not far."

"We know where we're going. We know what we *want*. But do we know the best way to get it once we're there?"

Ari was silent for a moment, pondering the words of a woman who had to be at least five years her junior. Ari admired Helia more every minute. She stole a glance at Helia but forced herself to avert her eyes as she responded.

"Well, we enter at the center of Hector's back office. I'd estimate that the *target* is about ten feet from the entrance. I know *where* it is, but I don't know *what* we're looking for."

Helia was quick to respond. She had already planned the entire series of events.

"You'll retrieve the information while I cover you. We don't know what we're looking for, so take everything. We'll sift through it afterward."

Ari stopped again to look at her, somewhat surprised at her arrogance. "You'll cover me? With what? That pea shooter you have strapped on you? If they're waiting for us — "

Helia interrupted, "Is anything preventing you from moving while you object?"

Ari, flustered, began to walk again. "Like I was saying, if they *are* waiting for us, that pea shooter isn't going to do anything. I have a taser, but I need to get close to use it."

"I have a knife, too," Helia objected somewhat sarcastically.

"A *knife?* These are professionally trained, armored soldiers. They'll have heavy artillery. We have a peashooter, a knife, and a taser. We're missing one thing."

"What's that?"

"A miracle."

Helia laughed at Ari's quick wit. "Listen, Ari, I'm a trained soldier too, and I'm going to accomplish my mission or die trying. It doesn't make a difference to me. But I'm telling you, the only way for us to succeed is to follow a plan. I know it's a lot to ask, but I'm going to need you to trust me. What do you have to lose? Like you said, you threw away your better judgment the moment you saved my life. No point in trying to follow it now."

"Humph," Ari grunted, unable to find a follow-up objection.

"I'm going to take that as consent. Like I was saying," Helia continued, "we move quickly. As soon as you're on the inside, you make your move toward Hector's hiding spot. Grab everything and return to the entry point so we can escape."

"But what if they're waiting for us?" Ari said, re-voicing her concern.

"I will handle everything else. I want you to remain focused. The only thing you need to worry about is retrieving what we came for. Nothing else. Is that clear?"

"But I don't know what we're trying to get."

"That's why you'll take everything. That's the only thing I want you thinking of. Is that clear?"

"I understand," Ari said submissively, wondering if it was her lot in life to be ordered around.

"Good. That's all I ask. Don't worry, it's going to be alright. We're here — are you ready?"

Ari looked up and noticed Helia was right. They had arrived. Helia asked whether they were ready to climb up and knowingly barrel toward their deaths. Ari knew they were waiting for them. She could feel it.

"I'm ready when you are," Ari responded with a shaking voice, struggling to sound courageous.

"Alright then, let's move."

The two made their way up a ladder to the hatch leading into Helena's Tavern. At the top, Ari paused.

"C'mon, move," Helia whispered.

Ari let out a long sigh and opened the hatch.

WHOOP, WHOOP, WHOOP!

***

The fugitives were inside! Officer John Harris sprang into action immediately.

"Green Unit, Orange Unit, I want you in the sewers now!" Harris barked.

The moment had arrived, and the truth of his leadership ability was going to be revealed. A series of crackling noises could be heard on Harris' Polycom.

"Green Unit deployed and on the move, sir."

"Orange also a go, sir."

The team reports rolled in. The units were in position, pressing toward the entrance to Helena's Tavern.

"Alright, teams, I want you to move — we want to put the pressure on fast. Get to the point of entry as soon as you can! I also want it reported if the two fugitives are spotted. Let's keep the lines of communication open!" Harris commanded.

"Yes sir!" shouted his team leaders.

Harris turned his attention above ground. "Roof, East, West, and South Units, power up your heat scopes! I don't want to move in until we have a lock on their position. And remember, we take them alive!"

He was met with an affirmative response. Harris proceeded to do the same. He powered on a wrist monitor that was linked to the heat sensors. They operated on a unique band to avoid public interference or observation. Harris's face lit up from the glare of the LCD screen, lighting the beaded perspiration on his brow. He was afraid, exhilarated, and alert. His eyes darted intently, awaiting a lock on the objects within Helena's Tavern. Two dots with their coordinates emerged. One was stationary, while the other moved about the screen.

"Alright! We got two on-screen; does everyone have a read on them?" Harris barked.

"Yes, sir!" the squadron leaders responded.

"Alright, let's move in. Roof Unit take the lead, followed by West, East, and South. Is that clear?"

"Yes, sir!" was the unified response again.

"On my mark. Ready? NOW!"

***

"Shit! I knew it was a trap!" Ari yelled at Helia.

"Don't stop. Keep moving. You know what you have to do!" Helia snapped back.

As Helia removed her mask, the stench of pheromones assaulted her. She knew they didn't have much time. Ari, wounded by the sharpness of Helia's orders, jumped into action. The whooping of the alarm rang in her ears as Ari made her way through the cluttered office. Ari was accustomed to spending a lot of time in this space listening to Hector talking about the injustices of the world. The condition of Hector's office was a far cry from how Ari was used to seeing it. It was a disaster. Hector abhorred clutter. The chaos and mess of his most loyal patrons' lives compelled Hector to live in pristine order and cleanliness, or so Ari thought.

Ari was typically inebriated when she accompanied Hector to his back office. After her shift, Ari was usually the first to arrive and the last to leave Helena's Tavern. Hector tried to express a concern once or twice — he was a kind man. Ari remembered she had snapped at him too often, accusing Hector of acting like the government, trying to control her. Ari now realized why that retort always ended

Hector's efforts. As a Mutant sympathizer, he must have hated the government as much as she did and equating them must have offended Hector at the deepest level. As Ari rummaged, a smile passed across her face as she remembered her friend's kindness, concern, and sensitivity. The reflection rushed past her in a way that can only happen when one looks back on a memory. She remembered perfection and forgot flaws.

As Ari navigated through the office, she struggled to remember the layout. The previous landmarks lay strewn about, leaving the walnut walls bare. Heads of various statues and trophies stared skyward as Ari stepped through them. Ari was careful not to tread on them, irrationally fearing they might yell out in pain.

Alright, Ari. Think! Where did Hector always go to store his secrets? Ari thought to herself. Her head was on a swivel. Her eyes darted throughout the room, scanning the nooks and crannies of the space.

Observing Ari's behavior, Helia yelled, "No time for sightseeing. It's time to move!"

Great, I'm risking my life for her, trying to concentrate, and I'm getting yelled at, Ari thought, nodding in Helia's direction. *Now, he always went to the eagle's head which was mounted over the —* Ari paused as she noticed Hector's eagle head on the floor. She worked her way back to a gash on the walnut wall where it must have been mounted. Ari sprang into motion, knowing her destination.

Making her way with purpose, Ari threw aside any obstacle blocking her path. She paused, clearing the clutter on top of the false mantle Ari had seen Hector open many times before. Ari scanned her memory, trying to remember how Hector had opened it. The swirled scenes of her memory flowed like liquid before her mind's eye. *How did he do it?* Ari remembered there was a spot in the mantle. Ari fumbled over the surface of the hand-carved wooden molding. After probing and searching, a piece of wood moved under her touch. Ari grabbed it. Sliding it back, Ari found a keyhole. *A keyhole? I don't remember Hector using a key.*

"C'mon, Ari. What's taking you so long?" Helia yelled nervously, wondering why they had not encountered any Department of Sanitation officers when alarms sounded around them.

The Eagle! It suddenly clicked. Ari remembered Hector always fondling the bird before opening the compartment. He'd tickle its chin and say, "How is my night watchman doing?" or something like that. Ari moved back to the eagle's head as it lay wide-eyed with an open mouth.

"What are you doing? Do you have it?" Helia yelled.

Ari continued picking up the head, ignoring her, looking under its chin for a key. A flash of pink caught her eye. She reached into the mouth of the eagle and pulled out its tongue. It came out easily, revealing the metal glimmer of a key. Discarding the eagle head, Ari moved towards the mantle. Shoving the key and twisting in one swift motion, she slid the mantle lid open, revealing a series of storage devices, tubes, and folders. Ari gathered everything in her arms. She looked at the debris at her feet, found some fabric she could use as a makeshift sack, bundled the contents of Hector's safe, and rushed back to Helia.

Helia knew they didn't have much time. Their attackers were about to strike. The stench assaulted her from every direction. She turned and saw Ari rushing towards her, holding a sack. "I got it! Let's get out — "

CRACK!

The ceiling caved in, followed by a team of Department of Sanitation officers. Helia, on alert for any movement, was quick to react. Unsheathing her knife, she flew into action. The collapse of the ceiling created an air vacuum that sucked the loose clutter in Hector's office into the air. Paper swirled, reducing visibility. With her knife in hand, Helia vaulted off the ground. Searching for exposed flesh, she began to carve at the air with the precision of a laser. Helia felt projectiles whiz by her. She was in full attack mode, skin bristling with piloerection. She could sense the approach of any advance long before it struck. Officers dropped to the floor as Helia slashed anything her knife could pierce. She felt the splitting of skin and the warmth of blood covering her hand.

***

Hearing the cries of his officers over his Polycom, Harris forgot his strategy and rushed into Helena's Tavern. Barreling inside, he was caught in a swirl of chaos. Officers writhing on the ground, blood seeping from their armor. The floor of Helena's tavern was stained black and red. Harris tried to locate the mutant source of the anarchy. He saw a black blur at the center of the commotion. Moving closer, Harris made out the Mutant he had apprehended, dancing fluidly amongst his soldiers. One by one, his officers dropped as she spun and lunged at her victims with the speed of a viper. She defied gravity as she slashed, striking at any weakness in their armor. The officers were in disarray. They shouted and tried to shoot the deadly Mutant. Rubber bullets flew, striking other officers as she calmy danced out of their way. Harris noticed the Mule in standard issue, staring just as dumbfounded as himself at the Mutant. A moment of recognition passed between the two. Mouths agape. Stunned into inaction.

Harris shook himself from his trance and yelled into his Polycom. "Green and Orange Units, we need you from underneath! Move it!"

Within seconds, the subterranean entrance to Helena's Tavern burst open, and reinforcements spilled into the battle.

***

Ari jumped back. Their escape route burst open. A steady flow of Department of Sanitation officers rushed into Helena's Tavern. The action happened all around her. She felt helpless. Ari watched motionless as Helia contorted in mid-air. Her arm struck methodically, lashing out and striking with lightning quickness. Blood flowed, marking the spots she hit. Helia never missed. Everywhere she struck, an officer collapsed. It was almost as if her knife was a red paintbrush. With the ease of an artist, she left her mark on her canvas. The officers' attention was focused on her. Holding the sack motionless, Ari felt invisible. She wasn't much more than a filing cabinet. Still and unmoving, an inanimate piece of furniture. Up to that point, Ari had thought they would have made it. But with the reinforcements, where could they go? How would they get out of this situation?

***

Helia felt alive. This was what she was meant to do. She could feel the adrenaline coursing through her veins. Every gleam of flesh was rewarded with a strike of her knife. Her feet kicked the walls, ledges, chairs, or anything that would change her direction in mid-flight. She knew she couldn't touch the ground lest she be tackled. She kept moving elusively, tickled by the projectiles flying past her. Helia could feel they were going to make it. She had done enough damage that they were going to be able to make a break for freedom. She was twisting to get behind Ari and rush toward the exit that was their entrance just moments ago. When Helia glanced down, their escape route erupted. Officers flooded the tavern. She knew what she had to do.

***

Harris drew his gun and started blasting round after round of rubber bullets. His automatic pistol held three rounds of twelve bullets. The shells were released in bursts, and if he kept his finger on the trigger, they would continue firing until he had exhausted his ammunition. He had additional rounds. They could be quickly loaded into his pistol with his alternate hand and would lock in for non-stop firing action. His target was the Mutant. He fired relentlessly to no avail, cursing himself and the Mutie every time he missed.

"Damn it! Why won't you stay still long enough for me to hit you?" he cursed.

Harris stopped, realizing the abrupt silence. He tried to yell orders to the troops. He felt his mouth move, but no sound escaped. Harris watched the silent chaos. The blasts from his gun sent waves of shock down his arm, but each discharge was silent. Harris surveyed the scene. All his units were accounted for. Hundreds of officers were firing openly at their target, but he couldn't hear a thing. Harris thought he may have gone momentarily deaf, assuming the noise may have burst his eardrums, but there was no ringing. No, it wasn't just him. His officers began to pause. They looked at each other, utterly confused by the eerie silence that enveloped them.

Harris made eye contact with Sheik, who had taken off his helmet to see if that was the source of the anomaly.

"Can you hear anything?" Harris yelled.

Sheik shook his head at Harris, pointing to his ears, mouthing.

"Can't hear you!"

Panic struck his officers. Harris saw it in their eyes. He tried to scream orders, but half of them had stopped their pursuit of the Mutant. Confusion, fear, and doubt started to infect them all.

Harris felt the walls of failure begin to close in on him. He wasn't going to sit idly. He reloaded his gun and tracked the Mutie. She was just about to touch the ground behind the Mule.

Good, two with one shot. The Mutie's a damn coward using the Mule as a shield, Harris thought to himself.

He let loose with his gun. Following their commander's lead, Harris' fellow officers did the same, silently screaming their aggression toward the two.

***

It was time. Her years of training provided the time and environment to hone her Mutant abilities. Helia collected the waves of sound and motion using the chaos that swirled around her. She could feel the energy course through her, channeling it into a singular focus. She stole the sound and motion out of the room. The air became thick. Everything slowed. Helia saw the look of panic through the eye slits of the faceless helmets worn by the Department of Sanitation officers. Helia twisted toward Ari, who stood motionless and confused. Feeling the ground touch beneath her, she landed behind Ari. Leaning forward, she whispered, "Now I'll need you to protect me."

***

Ari stood in the center of the chaos, dumbfounded. She couldn't hear anything. It felt as if she was in the eye of a storm. It almost made the chaos tranquil. Ari looked around. Department of Sanitation officers were looking at each other in confusion. Some took off their helmets to scream inaudibly at each other. From their reactions, Ari could tell they were experiencing something similar. Their eyes were full of fear. They looked at each other for reassurance. Ari watched Helia dance gracefully in the air, defying gravity as she moved toward her. She felt the floor vibrate under her feet as Helia landed behind her. Ari's heart began to race as she felt Helia's body close to hers. She looked forward and, for the first time, became afraid. All of the officers were staring directly at Ari, pointing their firearms in her direction. Things seemed to slow. She saw the soldiers jerk from the recoil of their weapons firing. She could see the bullets flying in her direction. From behind, she felt the warm breath of Helia tickle her ear.

"Now, I'll need you to protect me."

Helia's voice made Ari's heart jump into her throat. The soft whisper broke the silence that enshrouded Helena's Tavern. Helia's arms thrust in front of her, embracing Ari from behind. Ari turned her eyes toward Helia's hands and watched the scene before her bend. The air warped in front of Ari, creating an invisible wave that distorted everything. The wave fanned outwardly from Helia's hands, making Ari and Helia the eye of the storm. As the wave traveled, it deflected bullets mid-flight. Ari watched as the bullets scattered harmlessly away from them. Horror struck the faces of the Department of Sanitation Officers. They helplessly watched the wave move toward them, momentarily distorting their faces. Their mouths screamed silently as it overtook them. Eyes burst, releasing fountains of blood. The officers who managed to loosen their helmets clutched at their eyes and ears to try and contain the gush of blood. As the wave moved, it released the sound it once consumed behind it. Ari's hair stood on end as she heard the blood-curdling cries of hundreds of officers as they fell. The floor-bound officers began to convulse as they entered the throes of death.

Ari felt the weight of Helia collapse on top of her. *Oh no. She's dead!* She thought. Turning around and dropping everything, Ari took Helia in her arms. Helia was breathing. Whatever she did must have taken a lot out of her. Ari turned back to look at the carnage. Hundreds of dead Department of Sanitation officers lay in a heap. Their bloodstained limbs intertwined. The whooping of the heat sensors broke her trance. Ari could hear the drones whiz outside, bleeping in confusion. The wave had shattered all the windows of Helena's Tavern as it had fanned out of the bar. Ari hoisted Helia over her shoulder. Knowing that the drones were outside, Ari made their escape the way they had come.

Once Ari had safely secured Helia below, she returned to retrieve their prize. Ari surveyed the scene. She found a chest plate wide enough to fit her and collected what weapons she could find, along with any unused ammunition. Ari loaded everything into a backpack she grabbed off a dead officer. Once she had finished looting, Ari returned to the sewer. She lifted Helia and made her way through the underground tunnels. Her second home. Ari knew a safe spot. A spot where Helia could heal and regain consciousness.

CHAPTER 6

Director Franco DeSouza overlooked the sleeping city from his office. He didn't go home that evening; he wanted to be close by when Officer Harris brought in the Mutie and the Mule. He looked forward to the interrogation. Besides, nothing was waiting for him at home. That change happened a long time ago. Even if he did go to his empty house, he wouldn't have been able to sleep. The director was a little on edge at having taken the risk of assigning Officer John Harris to lead the op. His instincts told him it was the right thing to do, and DeSouza always followed his instincts. But there was a doubt that boiled deep inside him. This was typical for DeSouza. It usually happened after any tough decision he made. DeSouza often second-guessed his judgment, but he knew he wasn't alone in this habit. Any decision that could have multiple outcomes brought his thoughts to the least-desired results becoming a reality. DeSouza would have been lying if he had told anyone he wasn't worried. There was no point in going home for a sleepless night while he awaited daybreak to find out whether his instincts were right.

DeSouza lived for his work. There was a time when he looked forward to being away from work, but that was many years ago. Back then, he had everything: a successful career in the Department and a wife who loved him. He was the envy of many of his peers. The most painful time of his life came at what should have been the most joyous. Arriving home after a long shift from work, his wife had prepared him his favorite meal. She had set three dinner plates at the table. DeSouza remembered that night vividly. It played in his head many times — another reason why he often avoided being home. The memories were more painful there, more haunting. His dining room had yellow walls with wood accents. It was an older home built in the early twentieth century, still having most of its original molding. The bright colors reminded him of his parents' house. The walls were decorated with pictures of their wedding. DeSouza enjoyed spending time in the dining room most — oh, the hours he'd spent there with his wife. Now he avoided it. Seeing three plates that night, he knew he was in for a surprise. His wife, Donna, liked to playfully test her husband. She always told him that if he was going to make Director, he had to keep his wits sharp. Donna felt it was her duty to be the grindstone that sharpened those wits.

DeSouza began the inquisition as soon as she entered the room.

"Expecting anyone?" he asked with a broad smile to let Donna know he knew the game was afoot.

"Why yes, yes I am," she replied slyly.

"Do I know this person?" DeSouza asked, beginning the process of elimination.

"Not yet."

"Okay, how did you meet this person?" DeSouza continued, getting more suspicious.

"Well, I was introduced quite suddenly last week."

"What does this person look like?"

"I don't know."

He looked at his wife, perplexed, his brow knitted, glaring suspiciously. He could see she was giddy with delight at his confusion.

"So, how do you not know what the person looks like if you met them last week?" DeSouza said, poking holes in her logic.

"I never saw them," Donna answered nonchalantly as if it made perfect sense that she hadn't seen the person who visited her.

DeSouza remembered being frustrated. He hated losing. In hindsight, it seemed silly not being able to figure it out. A moment he'd regretted.

"I think this person will keep you up quite late at night. But don't worry — that won't be for months."

"Months! Alright, I'm stumped. Who is it?"

"I'll give you a hint: this person will arrive in six months, but they started their journey about three months ago. I don't know what the person looks like, but I know they'll resemble both of us. They won't be much of a talker at first, but they'll come around after a while. And they're guaranteed to be as much of an inconvenience as possible. Still, I have a feeling we'll love them regardless." Donna finished with a satisfied glance. She knew the clues would be sufficient. DeSouza looked at his wife through teary eyes.

The memory of becoming a father overwhelmed DeSouza. The emotions threatened to overtake him.

"Uh, sir, are you there?" His intercom crackled.

DeSouza snapped out his fog. "Yes, I'm here."

"Sir, if you are in your office, please respond," the intercom crackled again.

"I'm here, damn it!" DeSouza yelled. But he hadn't activated his mic. Scrambling back to his desk, DeSouza slammed the button on his intercom.

"I'm here. What is it?"

"Sir, we've lost all communications with Harris' units."

"What? Report!" DeSouza barked.

"Sir, we lost communication and activity with all units about ten minutes ago. And we've determined it is not a technical problem," the crackling voice reported.

"Explain."

"Well, at first, sir, we thought we might have lost a comm cell. But after some testing, we determined that was not the case."

"What about the drones deployed in the region? Can you get a video feed from them?"

"We tried, sir. The drones confirmed that we didn't have a comm cell problem, but they're having trouble with the relay."

"What do you mean, officer?"

"We can see the drones on screen. We're tracking their movement. They are somewhat functional, but we can't remotely connect to any of them or get a feed.

"Alright, let's deploy some new drones into the battle scene. I want to know what's happened."

"Already deployed, sir. We should be getting some information streamed back to us within the next couple of minutes."

"Who am I speaking to?"

"Officer Mercado, sir."

"Good, Mercado. I'll be down in the Operations Center in a minute; I want to be there when the data comes in."

"Understood, sir."

DeSouza cut the transmission. He buried his face in his hands, mind racing. He was convinced that Harris had failed horribly and was already blaming himself. DeSouza should have known better than to send out Harris as the point man. He'd been a beat officer for too long. He didn't have what it took to lead.

DeSouza rose from his chair and made his way toward the door. He turned around to look at his peaceful office. He imagined it would be the last time it would look peaceful for a while. There were going to be weeks of fallout because of his failure.

***

DeSouza flinched as the security scanner attempted to scan his retinas.

"Error. You must have your eyes open for a successful verification," informed a computerized voice. DeSouza would never get used to this. He placed his fingers over his eyes and widened them forcefully to ensure they would not close again. He felt the red light pierce his vision, verifying his identity.

"Thank you, Director DeSouza. Please proceed," the computerized voice replied. The door to the OC slid open to reveal what was affectionately referred to as the fish tank: the glass-encased Operations Center.

The Operations Centre was the nerve center for the Department of Sanitation with live feeds streaming in from all parts of Cincuenta Yuno. It was staffed around the clock with officers who observed the incoming video. The OC consisted of a series of LCD screens with twenty terminals. The LCD screens displayed multiple feeds throughout the city. Any drone that registered an abnormal occurrence would take priority and immediately pop on screen. Officers on duty could pull up a feed from any active drone surveillance camera or heat sensor through their terminal and share footage with the ops teams.

The OC was an airtight environment with no windows to ensure that the information inside would be protected if the OC was under attack or on fire. A chemical would be released that sucked away all oxygen, which would put out any type of fire. In the case of a chemical release, officers on duty would have to evacuate immediately or die from asphyxiation. The OC was underground, encased in lead and concrete. It could withstand the force of a nuclear explosion and was designed to prevent any external gas or radiation from seeping in. It stored *all* of the data for the Department of Sanitation. Information regarding officer reports, interrogation results, criminals, private citizens, Mules, Mutants, and results of new weaponry testing — the data was endless. If the department lost the OC, it would lose everything it had recorded, dating back to pre-war times. Backups were taped and shipped to another storage facility in another district. But tapes could be lost or damaged. And if unsaved data got lost before a tape backup, that data would be lost forever. DeSouza remembered a time when districts were connected through fiber networks. Those connections had long since been severed ever since the war.

The officers on duty were quite different from Officer DeSouza. They stayed in the dimly lit OC while on shift, so their eyes were always wide and red from looking at the screens around the clock. They had to be reasonably adept at troubleshooting technical failures in the server stacks or the field. Known for their unique culture, the OC officers tended to have wry humor and a sense of superiority. They had phrases taped onto the bulletproof glass of the fish tank reading, 'Please do not feed the animals,' or, 'Please adopt one of us. We're housebroken.' The officers usually referred to themselves as seers. They saw everything and held a strong disdain for other officers in the Department of Sanitation.

DeSouza entered the OC and was met with several suspicious eyes. Only three agents were on duty. The pale-skinned, red-eyed faces watched him intently. Realizing DeSouza's identity, they awkwardly got to their feet, saluting. It was a new experience for the OC, a place DeSouza avoided. He did not like the officers in the fish tank. They usually spoke to him in a condescending tone and made sarcastic remarks that generally went over his head. DeSouza valued their role in the department but didn't consider the OC inhabitants to be real officers. DeSouza was a man of action. He prided himself on bringing order out of chaos and being at the center of it all. The OC officers were always on the sidelines, judging from afar. Still, DeSouza knew who they were and recognized Mercado immediately.

DeSouza began barking orders, not wanting the OC officers to have a chance to judge his presence or abilities.

"Mercado. Report. What do you have since our last conversation?"

"Sir," Mercado motioned DeSouza over to his terminal, "As you can see, you've just arrived for the show."

Mercado began typing at his terminal and brought up the streaming video on the main screen.

"We have just penetrated the perimeter of the zone sealed off by Officer Harris' operation. As you can see, the original drones deployed are behaving erratically, and the scene is uncommonly quiet."

DeSouza observed the feed. It looked like a deserted ghost town. Vehicles were abandoned, and doors were ajar. The windows of the neighboring establishments were all shattered. Drones whizzed by, slamming into walls.

"Can you speak through the drone?" DeSouza inquired, thinking it was a good idea to announce their presence.

"Sorry, sir. The drones are equipped with microphones, but they can't broadcast. It's a good idea, though," Mercado said reassuringly, nodding to his colleagues to take note. DeSouza wasn't appreciative.

"Well, let's get inside Helena's Tavern."

"But, sir, don't you want us to gather as much information about the perimeter as possible before going inside? If we lose this drone, it will take some time before we can have another on-site."

"Send it in. That's where the action is. I have hundreds of officers on this operation, and I don't know where any of them are. That's my priority," DeSouza snapped, disgusted at Mercado's disinterest in his fellow officers' wellbeing.

"Going inside," Mercado announced, working diligently to navigate the drone into Helena's Tavern.

Nothing in his years on the force prepared DeSouza for the sight he was about to witness. As the probe entered Helena's Tavern, a look of abject horror passed over the faces of the small group in the OC. DeSouza couldn't believe his eyes.

The carnage was unimaginable. Angular bodies of officers were piled on top of each other. The floor was stained with their blood.

"Wh — wha — what am I seeing here?" DeSouza stammered.

"Uh, sir, we are on the inside, and this is the live feed," Mercado replied timidly.

"Is it possible that someone has intercepted the feed to give us this image?" DeSouza asked hopefully. He couldn't accept what he was seeing.

"Williams, can you run a traceroute to determine if there are any interrupts along the path?" Mercado asked.

"Got it," a man with blond hair and dark bags under his eyes said as he turned his attention to his terminal, sneaking glances at the primary screen, unable to avert his eyes.

"Director, sir, the traceroute made each leg without delay. It's unlikely that anything could be intercepting the signal."

DeSouza saw a gleam of hope. "Unlikely?"

"Correct, Sir, about .009 percent possibility of a hack."

DeSouza frowned, knowing there was no need to put any weight into this remote possibility. "Is there any way of knowing who's down there?" DeSouza asked, beginning to accept the worst.

Mercado paused before answering, "We're not picking up any heat signatures. We can run facial recognition for officers without helmets. For others, we can begin collecting blood samples. The drone may be able to analyze the blood, then we could cross-reference the information against our officer database. But there's a high probability of cross-contamination."

"Make it happen," DeSouza ordered.

Mercado busied himself at his keyboard. After typing a few commands and receiving an error message, Mercado huffed. "Hmmm. Doesn't look like it'll work, sir. Too much cross-contamination for blood sampling. Moving in for facial recognition."

Two officers in the OC let out a gasp. DeSouza and Mercado lifted their heads to look at the screen. The probe passed over an officer who had managed to discard his helmet. His face was stuck in a final moment of terror and pain, mouth agape in a silent scream. His eyes had burst, leaving trails of blood that streamed down his face like tears. Rivers of red from his ears formed a large pool around his head. The room collectively shuddered.

"What could've done that?" the blond officer exclaimed in disgust, still reeling from the carnage. Most OC officers had never witnessed any sort of bloodshed.

DeSouza's mind began racing with possibilities. "Mercado, check the atmosphere for any foreign agents. Maybe this is the result of a chemical attack."

"Yes, sir." Again, Officer Mercado began typing frantically at his terminal. "Sir, the atmosphere is completely normal and breathable."

"Then what the hell could've done this?" DeSouza asked without expecting an answer.

"*DESOUZA!*" a voice barked from behind him.

DeSouza whipped around, and the OC officers followed. It was the Controller of Cincuenta Yuno, Derrick St. Jean. Taken aback at the Controller's presence, DeSouza stiffened up and saluted. "Controller, sir, what can I do for you?" a confused DeSouza asked.

"We have reports that hundreds of lives had been lost attempting to collar a Mutie. Is this true?" St. Jean snapped in his scruffy voice.

Controller Derrick St. Jean was roughly DeSouza's age. They had known each other for years: politics and law enforcement were often intertwined. A relic from years past, St. Jean was tall and broad. He had silver hair and slits for eyes. His pale face sagged, showing signs of age. He was only a shadow of the dashing young politician DeSouza remembered. Crow's feet had almost consumed his black, beady eyes, which still flashed with brilliance. Despite his worn appearance, he was a commanding presence. St. Jean maintained his broad and muscular physique. His muscles warped his conservative blue shirt. It was an odd contrast; he had a well-maintained form, but his face had seemingly melted with time.

Controller St. Jean was flanked by two bodyguards whom DeSouza knew well. They had both been officers under his command , leaving the force for the more lucrative position of guarding the controller full-time. DeSouza didn't respect the decision, but he knew they both had families, so he didn't begrudge them. The two imposing figures stood across from each other. They were almost mirror images. Their chiseled features and position behind the controller almost made them a reflection of his previous self. They shared short chestnut-colored hair and were equipped with high-tech glasses that enabled them to perceive objects by heat and infrared. Both bulged with muscles, making it seem unlikely for them to move with any agility. DeSouza noted that each carried a .45 caliber kick-barrel piece and a multi-round blaster with various options: spray, hammer, and rapid fire. Plus, laser sights and quick loading action. That was just what he could see. Who knew what else the artillery geeks had developed?

DeSouza frowned. The Department never received the lethal weaponry that high-level government agents did. They were reduced to using rubber bullets and tasers for their beat cops. Out in the desert, their covert officers received outdated hand-me-downs from the higher levels of government. Sure, they were still effective, but they were known to jam and sometimes backfire. DeSouza would like to see his department better equipped.

Controller St. Jean was responsible for overseeing the functions of all of Cincuenta Yuno. He was DeSouza's boss, although they rarely communicated. Since being promoted to the directorship, DeSouza had only spoken to St. Jean once, which was at his swearing-in. St. Jean oversaw many Departments: Sanitation, Security, Essential Services, Trade, and Commerce. He *was* Cincuenta Yuno, and his visit didn't bode well for DeSouza.

"Yes, sir! We have a Mutie infiltration, sir!" DeSouza answered. He knew there was no point answering the question indirectly or elusively. St. Jean's information was superior to his, so he might as well give him everything he knew.

"Sir, we lost contact with all units about forty minutes ago. They were deployed to collar a Mutie. The infiltration of Cincuenta Yuno occurred via the sewage system. She has been aided by a conspiring Mule whose file number escapes me right now. I do have it in my office. The Mutie was returning to an establishment named Helena's Tavern, where we had brought in a suspected Mutie conspirator."

"Where is the conspirator now?" St. Jean interrupted.

"He was interrogated, sir," DeSouza replied.

"I see. Continue," St. Jean requested.

Turning his attention to the LCD screens, DeSouza continued.

"What you see behind us looks like all deployed units on the operation... no survivors." DeSouza could see the two bodyguards wince at the images onscreen. There were no regrets from either of them for leaving the force. St. Jean looked at the screen and paused, thinking.

"DeSouza, you have done a fine job up to this point," St. Jean spoke slowly.

"Thank you, sir," DeSouza responded submissively, anticipating the following words.

"I'm taking over this issue and appointing an interim director to fill the vacancy."

DeSouza looked down in shame. He averted his eyes from everyone in the room.

"Am I to pack my things and turn in my issue, sir?" DeSouza asked, trying to sound strong.

"No, DeSouza. Look at this as temporary. You can appreciate my position, I'm sure."

"Yes, sir," DeSouza responded.

"Hundreds of agents lost their lives today, and someone has to take the fall. You gave the order; you take the blame."

"Understood, sir."

"I'll still need you and your expertise, though. I want you to run point with my security lead. Your experience will be invaluable."

"Anything I can do to help, sir." DeSouza couldn't help sounding defeated.

"Alright, I want you to gather all the information regarding this case and report to my office at zero-eight hundred hours. In the interim, I will get Essential Services to bring in the dead and quarantine the area. There may not be an airborne chemical released, but *something* did this. We also need to start contacting the next of kin regarding the fatalities."

"Yes, sir," DeSouza responded. "I'll be ready to report by zero-eight hundred hours."

"Good, don't worry about clearing out your office. I'll arrange everything — I'll have to announce your dismissal as director by noon tomorrow. Until then, use your rank and office in any capacity necessary to put together the report."

"Yes, sir. Mercado, I want compressed footage provided to me within the hour," DeSouza said, snapping back into action.

"Yes, sir," Mercado responded, relieved that some normality had returned to the situation.

"I'll take my leave now, DeSouza. There's a lot to prepare for," St. Jean said. Then, he turned and walked out of the OC, followed by his two guards, who still wore an expression of shock. After the controller had left with his entourage, DeSouza slammed his fists on the desk. The OC was silent, the air thick with tension.

"Alright, I'll be in my office — and I'll be expecting that footage. Mercado, I may contact you periodically for my report. How long are you scheduled on shift?" DeSouza asked.

"I'll be here until you no longer need me, sir," Mercado responded.

"Perfect."

DeSouza turned, shaking his head as he made his way to the door. He paused before leaving as if to say something but left the OC silent.

CHAPTER 7

DeSouza returned to his office distraught. The gravity of so many deaths weighed heavily on him. He fell into his chair, defeated. His demotion just compounded his feeling of failure. He buried his face in his hands and rubbed his temples. The pain of the day could not be erased. Losing Baisley was tough. Now, he wished that only one officer had been a causality. Instead, the blood of hundreds stained his hands. *How could this have happened?* DeSouza asked himself.

DeSouza looked out the window of his office. It was the first time he felt happy that Donna was gone. He wouldn't want her to witness this failure. Let alone his unborn child, whom he felt he had failed too. DeSouza remembered the frequent doctor's visits during his wife's pregnancy. Everything was so positive until they reached the last trimester. Doctor Weiss had pulled them aside and asked for a confidential visit. DeSouza hadn't thought much of it at the time. He remembered thinking it was probably to consult on delivery methods, the types of drugs available, or the pros and cons of natural childbirth. But the conference went quite differently.

Doctor Weiss was always very kind to the DeSouzas. He spoke slowly, in a sing-song manner that had a soothing tone. He had been delivering children for over twenty years. That fateful day, Weiss brought them into his office and motioned them to sit down in front of his desk. DeSouza found the formality odd. It wasn't consistent with their previous meetings. His department instincts started to kick in, sensing an impending danger. Donna began crying immediately, feeling the same. DeSouza rubbed his wife's back, attempting to console her, growing furious that Doctor Weiss didn't do anything to calm her concerns.

"Weiss, could you please tell my wife that there isn't anything to worry about!" DeSouza snapped.

"I wish I could," Weiss began softly in his usual manner as he looked over his horn-rimmed glasses. Weiss must have been one of the last humans to wear glasses instead of correcting his vision with laser surgery. His face was wrinkled, and his head was bald and discolored with spots. His thick, broad hands were gentle as they removed his glasses.

"I'm afraid your child is *not* normal," Weiss began slowly, selecting his words carefully.

"What does that mean?" DeSouza barked, still trying to be in control.

"I'm sure you're aware of the recent government testing required for unborn children?" Weiss asked, knowing DeSouza was familiar with the tests and why they were done.

"Yes," DeSouza frowned. He knew what was coming; his child was a Mutant. It would have to be destroyed. They would then have to be sterilized to ensure they didn't produce any subsequent Mutant offspring.

"That's right, Franco. Your unborn child is… gifted and will have to be extracted immediately. Your wife is in the last trimester and will need to be operated on."

Donna sobbed uncontrollably. A dream shattered. Donna came from a large, loving family and couldn't wait to start her own.

"When does 'immediately' occur?" DeSouza asked in a sour tone as he rubbed the back of his distressed wife.

"Franco, Donna, this is happening more and more frequently. Any sterilization operation is reversible once our society becomes more open to the change that our species is undergoing," Weiss explained, trying to soothe the young couple's pain.

Weiss wasn't part of the conservative movement to eliminate Mutants, thinking it would somehow preserve Norm society. Although Weiss might not have looked like someone to embrace change, he was quite the opposite. Though he understood that society's acceptance of Mutants would not occur within his lifetime. Weiss hated bearing this sort of news. It wasn't unchartered territory. Earlier in his career, there were a number of complications that could occur. But he would always wrap ill tidings with hope. This news was much more devastating and final.

After a pause, Weiss continued. "As I was saying, this is happening much more frequently, and the hospitals are overrun with these operations. We are committed to performing the procedure promptly. Expect at least twenty-four hours' notification before the procedure. You will be notified within two months," Weiss finished. He stared intently at the DeSouzas, searching for clues in their reaction.

"I know it is a lot to take in. Do you have any questions?" Weiss asked.

The DeSouzas were in shock, still processing the information. The stolen future they had been dreaming of and planning over the past months was.

"I don't think we have any questions at the moment. But will you be available to answer any questions if they come up?" DeSouza asked.

"Of course, Franco, anything you need. I'll give you my home number as well." Doctor Weiss scribbled on a pad of paper and handed it to DeSouza.

"Thank you, Doctor Weiss, for all your help," DeSouza said, taking the his information.

"I wish *I could* be of more help," Weiss said, momentarily holding on to the paper with one hand and DeSouza's hand with his other.

"So do we, Doctor," DeSouza said, meeting Weiss' eyes. There was something behind his stare, but DeSouza couldn't process it, just noted it for later.

"Do call then, Franco," Weiss requested as he released DeSouza's hand and the information he was passing.

DeSouza didn't have much time to think about their exchange. He had to focus on Donna, who was convulsing with sobs. DeSouza helped his wife to her feet. He hugged her close, whispering comforting words to her. He escorted her out of Weiss' office and took her home.

***

In the days following their meeting, life was excruciatingly quiet in the DeSouza household. DeSouza went to work every day, but he was just going through the motions. Every night, he returned home in silence that continued throughout their dinners. Both had so much to say but were unable to talk. The words would be accompanied by too much pain. It was easier to just avoid it. They both feared the inevitable call, their time together feeling like pins and needles. Donna spent most of her days like DeSouza, going through the motions. She found herself crying uncontrollably whenever she caught a glance of herself in the mirror. DeSouza often came home to Donna sobbing as she rubbed her pregnant belly. Three weeks later, there was a knock on the door during dinner. They looked up at each other, fearing the worst.

Donna immediately burst into tears, stammering, "D — do you think it's them?"

"I don't know." DeSouza tried to sound calm, but his heart raced. He was more afraid than he'd ever been with the department. DeSouza rose from his seat and made his way to the door. He looked out the window. Standing alone was Doctor Weiss. DeSouza heaved a heavy sigh. "It's Doctor Weiss," he called to Donna.

Donna sprung to her feet and ran to hide. DeSouza watched his wife scatter and frowned. He knew this was going to be difficult. He opened the door, and before he could speak, Doctor Weiss began, "Franco, I'm glad you're home. We don't have much time!"

Taken aback by his urgency, he asked, "What do you mean, Doctor? I thought we were going to be given notice?" He snapped, wanting to prolong the inevitable.

"That's not what I mean, Franco. Can I come inside?"

DeSouza nodded. Weiss entered the house. DeSouza helped him take off his long, navy coat. Underneath, he was still in his scrubs. *He must have come straight from the office,* DeSouza thought to himself.

Doctor Weiss looked around. "Where's Donna? Is she here?"

"She ran off as soon as she heard it was you," DeSouza said.

"Of course, poor dear, this is all very traumatic," Weiss stated sympathetically.

"It's been very difficult since we found out," DeSouza remarked solemnly.

"No, I imagined it would be. Quickly, have a seat. We have much to discuss but very little time," the Doctor urged. "And please get Donna. She needs to be here."

Sensing the opportunity in the doctor's voice, DeSouza sat down and bellowed, "*Donna*! Come out! He isn't here to take you away. He's here to talk about something else!"

Donna appeared moments later, peering around the dining room corner, suspecting a trap. "Is that true, Doctor?" she asked through tear-swollen eyes.

"Yes, come, have a seat. I must speak with both of you."

Donna moved into the dining room and sat.

"What is it, Doctor?" DeSouza asked.

"I'll cut straight to the point. Do you want to keep your child?"

"*YES!*" Donna said, bursting into a fresh fit of tears.

"Of course, we would, but what's the meaning of this? We've been having a really tough time. I wouldn't want you to suggest something you can't follow through with," DeSouza warned.

"No, no, quite right, Franco."

"We'll do anything," Donna sobbed, "just tell us what we need to do."

"Hold on, Donna," DeSouza interrupted, nodding to Weiss to continue.

"It doesn't come without high sacrifice," Weiss warned.

"Dammit, Weiss, just tell us!" DeSouza demanded, losing his patience.

Weiss jerked to attention. His head checked the room as if he were concerned that there might be someone observing. He continued in a whisper. "There is a compound outside the city that takes in the parents of unborn Mutant children. If you're willing to leave this life behind, I can get you there," Weiss offered.

"*OH!* Franco, let's do it!" Donna exclaimed.

"Hold on, Donna. What do we have to do, Doctor?"

Weiss furrowed his brow. "I can only arrange for Donna to be escorted there."

The couple sat in silence. They averted their eyes and locked hands for comfort.

"I must remind you, I can't stay long. I fear I'm being followed, and if I am discovered, no one will be able to benefit from this arrangement."

"Okay, okay. Can you tell us why I can't go?" DeSouza asked.

"It's because you are an officer, Franco. I am taking a big risk here. I know you could arrest me right now. It would destroy the whole operation. I'm afraid they wouldn't be able to resist hunting these good people if you went missing. And I shudder to think what they might do to them."

DeSouza sighed. He looked at Donna and knew the answer she was hoping for, but the look in her eyes let him know this was his decision. Donna couldn't bear the thought of losing either of them. She couldn't be forced to make that decision…

"When do we have to let you know?" DeSouza asked.

"Sadly, right now. I know it is a horrible situation to be placed in, but it cannot be helped," Doctor Weiss explained quickly.

DeSouza knitted his brow. He had to make the most difficult decision of his life. He was used to making split-second decisions. It was part of his job. There was only one path that could open the door to having it all.

"We'll do it."

Donna began sobbing uncontrollably, throwing her arms around his neck. Tears streamed down DeSouza's face. "I figure if we stay, we'll never have a family. This will haunt us. We'll never be happy knowing we could have taken this option. But if you're out there with our child, there's hope. Plus, I can protect you from the inside, here. All I've ever wanted is to protect and provide for my family, even if that is a little old-school," DeSouza explained through tears.

Dr. Weiss nodded. "Someone will come to your home in the next week."

Doctor Weiss rose, eager to leave. He had lost the calm nature the DeSouzas had come to know. He grabbed his coat and began his exit.

"But Doctor, we have so many questions," DeSouza said, leaping to his feet.

"I know, Franco, but they will have to wait. I need to be on my way. Yours is not my only visit today. Don't worry. You will be contacted," Doctor Weiss explained. Weiss left the house. The door slammed shut on their fears and opened a world of possibilities.

The following week was a blur. So many emotions. The highs and lows of hope and loss tied into a knot. DeSouza knew they were making the right decision. The knock on their door eventually came. A tall young man with delicate features stepped into their home. This was the stranger they were trusting to help them risk everything for their family. He explained the process of Donna's escape. Donna was to be taken out of the city with a number of other expecting parents. They would stow away in a truck that supported some sort of supply chain. The envoy would rendezvous with a representative from the new society, who would take them the rest of the way. The driver would claim he was highjacked by Mutant marauders. To explain the disappearance of Donna, there had to be an "accident." Doctor Weiss would provide the necessary tissue samples to fool the authorities.

Executing the plan was the hardest part. Although the couple had discussed it for weeks, going over the details repeatedly, nothing could prepare them for their separation. They held each other, promising a quick reunion to dull the pain. DeSouza remembered his words. "I'll see you soon. Don't teach our child all of your bad habits. Leave some for me."

DeSouza went to work that day, visibly distracted. He did everything he could to ensure Donna had safe passage. He kept his ear to the wire, listening for any report of an escape attempt by Mutie-bearing parents. Nothing came up. He returned home to a fellow beat officer with helmet in hand, breaking the news that his wife had died in a fiery accident. The dental and DNA records confirmed as much. The words hit DeSouza. He knew this was all part of the plan, but hearing his wife had died aloud overwhelmed him. DeSouza collapsed and broke into tears. Although the news called for DeSouza to play the role, it was no act. His wife was gone. They spoke of hope, but DeSouza saw the possibility of the other side. A life of lonely despair. The worst pain came the following day.

The news was full of reports that a band of fugitives was apprehended on the city's outskirts and eliminated. They were said to be Mutie sympathizers trying to escape Cincuenta Yuno to breed a new species that would, one day, overthrow society. DeSouza's stomach dropped. Dizzy with nausea, he attempted to contact Doctor Weiss' office. The number had been disconnected. DeSouza looked up to the flashing screen: Weiss had been arrested on conspiracy charges. He was interrogated by Department officials. DeSouza knew it meant that Weiss was dead. Anguish rushed over him. He was hit by a tsunami of grief that pulled him out to a lonely sea. His suffering was gradually replaced with anger. He trusted Doctor Weiss, who promised the hope of having it all. But instead, DeSouza lost everything. His rage boiled to fury, which found a target: the sloppy Mutie sympathizers. He blamed them for not ensuring her safety, but he blamed *himself* for putting his wife in their hands. DeSouza cultivated an intense hatred towards Mutant sympathizers. They cost him his wife and child. Over time, he eventually began hating Muties, too. He rose through the department ranks and never allowed himself to love again.

CHAPTER 8

DeSouza wiped the tears from his eyes. The memories of his past always haunted him, but the present-day failure ushered him back.

"Alright, Frankie boy, clear your head. Time to focus," DeSouza said, trying to motivate himself.

"What could have caused that kind of carnage?"

DeSouza had never seen anything like that. He booted up his terminal to scour the archives. DeSouza began typing keywords, hoping to get a hit, something he could link to the assault on his department. He opened file after file. He found nothing. Most Mutant cases inside Cincuenta Yuno were isolated demonstrations of Mutie strength. The rare instances of officers dying at the hands of Mutants happened in close-quarter melee. Nothing he had witnessed or found through his research came close to the mass-casualty power of the scene back at Helena's Tavern. Based on the characteristics of the damage, all signs pointed to some sort of blast. DeSouza searched using the keywords "Mutant+weaponry." The search only revealed small weapons — zip guns, knives, and tasers. There was some evidence of artillery that must have been stolen from the department's covert operations, but nothing that could produce a blast that could kill hundreds. DeSouza contemplated the best way to find what he was looking for. *Maybe approach it from the symptom,* he thought to himself. DeSouza typed in the keywords "eyes+burst." After he pressed enter on his keypad, several promising search results appeared.

"Results of sound wave weaponry on test subjects."

"Sound wave impact to subjects eyes and ear drums."

"A new wave in weaponry."

DeSouza attempted to access the files. A password prompt appeared. He typed in his user ID and password.

"*Unauthorized access level. Available only to Department of Security level five or above,*" an error message said.

DeSouza leaned back in his chair, contemplating his next move. At least he had some idea of where to dig.

Did the Muties get their hands on some sort of sound wave blaster? Could the Department of Security be involved? DeSouza thought. After some contemplation, he pressed the button on his intercom, "Mercado, have you got those files ready for me yet?"

DeSouza waited for a response. Finally, a crackling voice could be heard, "Sir, just formatting now and getting ready to send."

"Good. I want you to deliver it personally to my office."

"But sir, there's only three of us on shift. We need double coverage at all times — it's protocol."

"Well, if one of your boys has to go to the washroom, tell him to pinch it. I'm still Director. I *am* the protocol around here, understood?" DeSouza felt less confident that he could throw his weight around, knowing that Mercado had witnessed the whole incident with Controller St. Jean. There was a silence for a moment. Finally, Mercado returned.

"Alright, sir, I'll be up momentarily," Mercado responded. He sounded uncertain.

"Good!" DeSouza barked, trying his best to sound commanding.

DeSouza had an ulterior motive for getting Mercado into his office. He hoped that Mercado could get him past the security. He needed to look behind the curtain. DeSouza compiled all the information from the "Hector" interrogations, Harris' work, and the information leading up to Hector's arrest.

DeSouza heard a knock at his door. "Yes?" he called out.

"Sir, it's Mercado. I have the files you wanted. I'm here to deliver it in person, as you requested." His last words sounded patronizing. DeSouza knew electronic delivery made more sense, but he needed help hacking the department systems, and he didn't want to request it over the intercom or in writing.

"Great, Mercado, come in," DeSouza called.

Mercado's head peeked in. He began to enter slowly, making his way toward DeSouza's desk, glancing suspiciously from side to side. Mercado's eyes were active. He was taking in all the information he could as he moved towards DeSouza's desk, noting the cold angularity of DeSouza's office.

"Have a seat, Mercado."

"Yes, sir," Mercado responded, taking a seat slowly. "Sir, just so you know, I don't think whatever happened back there was your fault. No one could have known." He paused, shaking his head, "I know what the Controller said, and I get it. I just wanted to let you know that we in the OC don't feel that way." Mercado finished, averting his eyes.

"Thanks, Mercado. But it *is* my fault. My officers' lives are *my* responsibility. Sure, I'm not certain anyone sitting in this chair could have avoided what happened back there. But I gave the order. What happened is on me. I'll have to live with that decision for a long time...." DeSouza said, trailing off almost absentmindedly. He shook his head to regain focus and looked intently at Mercado, who flinched from the eye contact.

"I *do* want you to know that I appreciate your words. I have a favor to ask, which is why I wanted you here in person. I need your help."

"Sir? What can I do?" Mercado asked suspiciously.

DeSouza told him about his research. Mercado listened intently.

"...which is why I need you to help me get access. I want to get my hands on that information," DeSouza said. Mercado paused and thought momentarily.

"You want me to hack in for you?" Mercado repeated.

"Yes, Mercado, I'm afraid that the Muties have gotten their hands on some sound wave weaponry. If someone on the inside has access to that, what happened back at Helena's may be just the beginning. The citizens of Cincuenta Yuno may not be safe."

"I see." Mercado paused, processing the information. "Sir, it sounds like you already have your information. Why do you want to hack in?" Mercado asked.

"Right now, it's just a hunch. I don't want to stand in front of Controller St. Jean on a hunch. I want to present hard facts," DeSouza explained.

"I understand," Mercado said. "Alright, let me take a look. I can probably get in." He moved behind DeSouza's desk. "Which files did you want access to?"

DeSouza pointed at the ones he had purposely left up on the screen. He rose from his seat and offered Mercado his chair. Mercado took the controls with ease, and began busying himself on the keyboard. He left Mercado in peace, sure that watching over his shoulder wasn't going to help. DeSouza walked to the window. He needed to clear his head and mentally piece together his presentation.

"You're in, sir."

DeSouza was surprised at how quickly Mercado was able to access the Department of Security files.

"That was fast!" DeSouza exclaimed, not afraid to show Mercado how impressed he was at his abilities.

"It was pretty easy, sir. Being the Director, you have high-level officer file access. I took a shot to see if you had access to any officers who'd moved to the Department of Security. Sometimes, HR forgets to eliminate access rights. Sure enough, you had access to any sanitation officer who'd moved over to the Security Department. It took a couple of tries, but I finally found the personnel with the right access privileges."

"You're a genius, Mercado!"

Mercado colored. "I loaded the files to your terminal. I didn't want to raise too much of a flag. Your terminal shouldn't be accessing any files with another login. The less time I was emulating another person, the better. Someone will still probably want to talk to you about it. I bet it's a pretty low priority. They probably won't get to you for a couple of days. By then, it might not matter." Mercado colored again, regretting his insensitive comment about the Director's forced resignation.

DeSouza nodded in approval. "Good work, Mercado. Thanks again for your help."

Mercado rose to give the Director his seat back.

"I also loaded the footage you wanted on your terminal. I put it all under a folder with today's date on your desktop."

Mercado stretched his hand out to DeSouza. "I wanted to let you know it has been a pleasure working with you, sir. I know we didn't interact much. You left the OC on its own. But that's exactly how we like to operate. The OC appreciated you because we hardly knew you were there, sir."

DeSouza met Mercado's hand and accepted the pseudo-compliment with a smile. After a final exchange of niceties, Mercado made his way out of DeSouza's office. He looked back at his Director one last time and closed the door.

CHAPTER 9

Ari felt the sewage rush through her feet as she made her way through the cavernous tunnels of Cincuenta Yuno. The smooth cement walls circling overhead echoed her movements. She had not been accustomed to moving in polycarbonate. It was the first time she had ever worn the material. It moved effortlessly with her body, but it still felt slightly constricting. The armor didn't breathe the way the fibers of her jumpsuit did. Ari felt overheated. The sack that contained their spoils hung heavy on her back. The weight pulled it away as if it were trying to break free. Ari couldn't adjust the sack because Helia was slung over her shoulder, still unconscious. She could feel Helia's body heave with long, drawn breaths. Ari was just relieved that Helia was breathing. She was making her way to a safe location where she could let Helia recuperate.

Winding through the dark tunnels, Ari marched towards her favorite location in the Cincuenta Yuno sewers. It was a landing located inside a large part of the pipe network perched halfway between the flowing sewage and the surface. Ari often spent time there whether it was to avoid work or submerge herself in thought. It was comforting there, especially when she felt particularly alone in the world. It was the only refuge she could escape to while she was on the clock. Ari knew they didn't have much time. It wouldn't be long before the Department of Sanitation regrouped and laid an all-out assault on the sewage system to find and kill them both. Ari had no idea what they were going to do. They had written their death certificates with the blood of the hundreds of officers who had died at Helena's Tavern. Ari was still reeling from what happened. She couldn't comprehend what she had witnessed. The warped faces that burst full of blood still haunted her. When she blinked, she could see more than a hundred faces with hollow eyes and open mouths screaming at her. Their faces streamed with blood. The sight made her shudder. She knew she wouldn't be able to forget it anytime soon.

Coming to an opening, Ari reached their destination. Working her way up a rusted ladder, Ari hoisted everything on top of the landing. It was the first time she had noticed how dangerous the ladder and landing were, but it was the first time she had something she wanted to protect. Ari could feel the ladder shake as she gripped each rung. She grabbed the ledge and felt the wire supports protruding from the eroded edge. Ari laid Helia down gently, cupping her head so she wouldn't hit it as Ari laid her down on the hard concrete surface. Ari reached into the sack and pulled out a halogen light she had snagged from the carnage. She lit it, illuminating the cavernous hub.

The light disturbed Helia. She began to stir. Ari moved in to ensure she didn't roll off the landing. She grabbed Helia's shoulders. "Now, be careful. You don't want to fall."

It was a poor choice of words. Helia immediately jerked her eyes open and tensed up, "Fall! What — "

Helia's eyes opened to see Ari crouching over her. She felt Ari's firm, gentle grip securing her. "What are you doing? What's going on?" Helia dazedly demanded.

Ari flushed with embarrassment. "You collapsed back at Helena's. We're in a safe place. It's an elevated platform here in the sewers. I thought we could rest here for a moment so you could get your strength back," Ari explained.

Helia's eyes rolled from side to side as she gained her bearings. "Oh, I see," she began. "Are you alright?"

"I'm fine. A little confused, but that's not new. I've been that way ever since we met."

Helia smiled. "I'm sorry you've gotten this involved. You're in so much danger." Her smile faded, quickly turning into a guilty frown.

"It's okay. Life was pretty dull until I met you," Ari confessed.

An awkward silence befell the two. Ari was the first to break the silence. "What happened back there?"

"I did what I had to so we could escape."

"But what *was* that?" Ari asked. "Do you have some sort of concealed weapon?"

"Well, I guess you can sort of say that," Helia replied, contemplating how best to explain.

"What do you mean? Can I see it?"

"You already have."

"I'm still confused," Ari said.

"You've been looking at it all this time."

"Not helpful."

"It's me. *I'm* the weapon."

Ari had trouble believing that Helia could be the vessel of such a destructive force. She seemed so small to her — slender limbs and soft skin. Helia felt Ari's eyes all over her and began feeling slightly uncomfortable. Ari flushed, noticing her body language. "But how could you — "

"I'm a Mutant soldier, remember?" Helia snapped, a little annoyed at Ari's lack of imagination. She couldn't blame her. After all, Ari was used to a Norm society where women were objectified. Nothing more than instruments for procreation or recreation for the Norm patriarchy. Even though Helia might look like a Norm woman, she wanted Ari to know better. After all, Ari was a powerful woman herself.

"But *how* do you do it?" Ari asked intently.

"I'm not entirely sure. We have scientists in our communities. They evaluate our abilities and recommend who is best suited for war. We train and explore our abilities in the Freelands." She continued, noticing Ari's uncertainty. "I know. It's hard to comprehend. I can also sort of tell what someone is thinking — "

"You mean you can read minds?" Ari interrupted, sounding a little worried.

"No, I can smell it. I guess that's the best way to describe it. People have different pheromones for different emotions, and just before they plan to do something, they release an odor. It's different, depending on what they plan to do."

"So, that's how you knew the two officers were at my place?"

"Yes. My skin is also very sensitive, especially when I'm excited. I can feel what people will do before they get a chance to do it. It's like the air warns me before anything touches me."

"Which is why you didn't get hit back there."

Helia nodded. "But the blast was the toughest thing to master. I spent months training, learning to channel that ability. I don't know what to call it. It's like I can gather all the motion and sound around me and condense it into an explosion. Air, noise, movement — it all produces something like waves. I just concentrate on collecting it from all around me until I feel swollen. It's very destructive when I release it. It takes a lot of energy, which is why I needed you to protect me. My trainers described it as my 'chi' or 'life force,' but I don't think so. It feels more external than internal."

"Does it hurt?"

"Not really. I get a massive head rush. Sometimes it's a lot to handle, and I can lose consciousness. I've never released that big of a blast. I've never been surrounded by so much activity in all my simulations. I was afraid for a moment that it was going destroy me."

"It was really scary. Did you know what it was going to do?"

Helia nodded, "I've seen the results in simulation. I know what a blast of that nature can do."

Ari, ashamed that she couldn't see Helia past her Norm prejudice, pressed on. "But have you actually *seen* what happens when you release a blast like that? You fainted right after."

"No, I guess not. I stay conscious during some of the smaller blasts — a little dizzy. Usually, they're more channeled blasts that send waves to a targeted area. From what I'm sensing from you, this must have been a big one."

"You killed hundreds of officers back there with a wave of your hands. Their eyes burst from the blast. I saw them struggle to escape the agony as their eyes spurted blood and their ears leaked like faucets. It was horrible," Ari said, clearly traumatized. A part of her was angry at Helia.

Helia stiffened. "I — I know it couldn't have been pretty, but you haven't seen what they've done to us out in the Freelands," Helia said defensively.

Ari sighed, "I know. No one's innocent here. But it's just — "

"Ari, once again, I'm sorry that you're involved. I wish it never had to come to this. If you want, you can leave any time."

"No, I can't! They know I'm involved! Not that I'd want to if I could… but I wasn't ready for anything like this. They were soldiers, just like you, doing their job. I think I was just looking for some remorse," Ari confessed. The idea of something was easier than its reality. Ari thought she would love kicking some Department of Sanitation ass. But seeing their lifeless faces was difficult. She had never killed anything. Even the vermin in her apartment she let cohabitate with her.

"I'm glad you're not leaving. You keep bailing me out of trouble. I wouldn't have made it this far without you." Helia smiled, placing her hands on Ari's.

Ari smiled back. She looked at Helia's soft, slender hand compared to her thick, strong one. It was such a contrast. "That's right. Now I'm up, two–nothing on saving your life," she said to Helia.

"What do you mean? I saved your life back at your home," Helia said, regaining some of her playfulness.

"True, but you also endangered it. They cancel each other out."

"Well, as long as you know me, your life is in danger, Ari. So, you can't keep using that as an excuse. You know what you're in for now."

"Yeah, I guess so," Ari admitted.

"Were you able to keep the items from Helena's, or did you have to leave them behind?"

"No, I brought them. I got some gear too."

"I noticed you found some body armor." She leaned forward and read Ari's chest plate, "Officer Harris," she said formally.

"Yeah, so don't make me take you in." Ari smiled.

"Let's see what we've got," Helia said eagerly.

CHAPTER 10

Having loaded his presentation, DeSouza stood in the dark meeting at the head of a long, cherry-colored table surrounded by unfamiliar faces. Real or imagined, he felt hostility from their glares. DeSouza couldn't see Controller St. Jean. He assumed that he must be sitting somewhere amongst the shadows.

"Please begin, Director DeSouza," a voice rang from somewhere in front of him. The projector began, and the lights dimmed, completely engulfing those seated around the table in darkness. The light blinded DeSouza, making it difficult for him to look in the direction of his audience. He turned to the screen and introduced his presentation.

"As you all know, the Department of Sanitation has recently experienced a severe tragedy. We have lost over one hundred and fifty agents during an operation led by the late Officer Harris. The operation was to apprehend a mole Mutant and her Mule accomplice. Assembling a swat team of veteran officers, Harris hoped to apprehend the duo in a surprise attack. All the officers were lost in the line of duty. You will see some footage of the aftermath. This presentation will provide you with the information leading up to yesterday's tragedy, hopefully enabling me to recommend a course of action for Controller St. Jean's review. Now, if there aren't any questions, I would like to proceed." DeSouza paused.

After a sufficient amount of time had elapsed, he continued. He shared all the information he had gathered from his research the night before. DeSouza explained how Hector fell under suspicion of being a Mutie sympathizer and the events leading up to his arrest, the information they'd gathered while Hector was under surveillance, Hector's interrogation, and DeSouza's suspicion of his untrustworthy testimony. This, he explained, prompted him to dispatch officers Harris and Baisley to stake out Helena's Tavern. DeSouza reported the death of young Baisley and his decision to put Harris in charge. Of course, he left out the human element innate to his decision-making. Instead, DeSouza focused on Harris' near single-handed apprehension of the Mutie. He explained that Harris was his most senior officer, who knew the streets of Cincuenta Yuno better than anyone in the department. As DeSouza listed his reasons for placing Harris in charge, he worried he had begun to sound defensive. His voice cracked, and he moved to show the footage of the aftermath of the encounter at Helena's Tavern. The carnage was highlighted, showing the digital images that the probe had relayed. Murmurs could be heard as the audience theorized about the source of such destruction. DeSouza capitalized on the conjecture and led straight to his conclusion.

"These symptoms have been seen before. The Department of Security has experimented with sound wave weaponry in the past. Although the results were quite effective, the department has not been able to produce a reliable weapon that could be used in combat. The research has been discontinued." Images from the files Mercado helped support DeSouza's hypothesis. He was pleased with its effect. The murmuring from his audience told him that it was new information.

"In conclusion, it seems as if the Mutants have been able to harness this type of technology effectively enough to cause wide-scale destruction. The results speak for themselves. This is the first indication that Mutants are gaining the capacity to pose a true threat to our Norm way of life. Previously, they had only been known to attack in small bands with zip guns, knives, and occasionally, department weaponry that had either been discarded or stolen. This signifies a marked change in Mutant aggression and capabilities. We must mobilize an attack unit and assault any known Mutant compounds. Eliminate the threat before they become one."

DeSouza's words silenced the murmuring of his audience. A sense of urgency could be felt in the room. Tension filled the air and the quiet became unbearable. DeSouza couldn't stand it. "That concludes my presentation. I would be glad to field any questions you may have."

"Thank you, Director DeSouza. Your report was very comprehensive. I will take over from here," the voice said.

The lights came on. The controller, as DeSouza suspected, had been sitting at the opposite end of the table, watching the presentation. DeSouza could take better stock of his audience with the room fully lit. Some of the faces were familiar. He recognized two officers who had worked with the Department of Sanitation before transferring to the Department of Security. Officers Foglia and Luis sat erect and stern-faced as they looked at their previous boss. DeSouza glanced around the table. There were twelve men, including the controller, gathered around.

"Director DeSouza," the Controller began. "Around this table, there are eleven hand-picked agents. Allow me to introduce them. Beginning clockwise from the left of you, we have Agent Tarrick."

DeSouza turned to take notice of the body sitting closest to him. Agent Tarrick was broad, freckled, and pale. His muscles had usurped his neck, making it near invisible. His hair screamed with fire-red tones. There was an eager glint that twinkled behind his emerald green eyes. His lips were thin slits, and his nose had been visibly broken several times. It zig-zagged from his brow to his lip. He was wearing a black suit, black shirt, and black tie.

Tarrick was known by most of his peers as the muscle in the Department of Security. He fearlessly followed orders. His reputation for being able to withstand physical trials dates back to when he was a cadet. Tarrick was hazed relentlessly. His tormenters tried to break the young cadet with punishing cruelty, forcing impossibly dangerous tasks upon him. Tarrick was able to withstand any punishment and complete any assignment, no matter how ridiculously dangerous, with ease. Eventually, Tarrick's hazers tired of the game. Their change of heart coincided with the realization of what Tarrick might do if *he* tired of their games.

"To his left, we have Agent Kim," Controller St. Jean continued.

Kim was of Asian descent. Like Tarrick and the other agents around the table, he was dressed in a black suit. Agent Kim was known for his versatility. Most of his peers called him Jack because he was a jack of all trades.

"Moving on, we have Agents Foglia and Luis. You should be familiar with them, DeSouza. They were in your department before they transferred over to security," St. Jean explained unnecessarily.

Both nodded and smiled. It was the first sign of warmth that DeSouza had felt since he entered the room. He knew both agents well. He used to be very close to Luis. They shared a Caribbean heritage. On the force, DeSouza had taken Luis under his wing. He thought of Luis as a younger version of himself. It was evident early on that Luis was destined for a different path. Luis scored quite highly on all his aptitude tests. DeSouza was an intelligent agent, but Luis was a genius. He proved to be a master strategist, and DeSouza knew he couldn't keep him long.

Foglia, on the other hand, was no genius. DeSouza thought him out of place. The only word DeSouza could really ascribe to Foglia was "genial." He was well-liked on the force. He wasn't an outstanding officer but had mastered the people skills necessary to motivate others. He also was quick to act and took control of situations easily. A born leader, he didn't bite off more than he could chew. Instead, he delegated responsibilities to those who were more talented. DeSouza smiled at the memory. Maybe he and Foglia were more alike than he thought. They shared a similar core quality: the ability to recognize talent and harness it.

"Agents Palmer and Dean Norton," the Controller continued.

DeSouza knew the twins too, sharing dark hair and eyes. They were inseparable.

"You know me, of course, and to my left is Agent Dalembert. He will be leading the operation," St. Jean explained.

Dalembert had small, weasel-like features. His beady black eyes glistened with intelligence. Dalembert's hair was slicked back, adding to his greasy appearance. He flashed a tight-lipped smile that stretched around his pointy nose, which turned up, mocking those who sat across from him. Dalembert was an excellent agent. He was a brooding strategist and an expert at stealth attacks. He often seemed distracted and aloof to most of his peers. However, he was known as relentless and invaluable in the line of duty. DeSouza didn't like him at all. His instincts screamed that Dalembert would be trouble.

"Rounding out the table, we have Agents Gooding, Franklin, Thompson, and Yusuf." They all nodded at DeSouza.

"We're gathered here today because of the recent events detailed in DeSouza's presentation. These events have warranted the immediate deployment of this special unit to search out and capture the rogue Mule and Mutie mole. We needed our best to conduct a targeted stealth operation. We now know the brutality of what we're dealing with. We must preserve our resources. This could be part of a larger Mutie strategy. And if so, we need to be able to defend Cincuenta Yuno from external Freeland attacks. Agent Dalembert has been put in charge of this operation and will receive full support from all of you. I will let him take over the meeting from here. Before I leave and let you work, know that we expect quick results. This cannot fester. I expect this matter to be cleared up within forty-eight hours. Anything less will be viewed as a failure. Agent Dalembert will answer any questions you may have. Good day, gentlemen." St. Jean finished, rose to his feet, and left the meeting room.

Silence fell. DeSouza noticed the dark cherry wainscoting baseboards that contrasted the hunter green walls. Abstract artwork hung strategically throughout the room. The north side had a wall with floor-to-ceiling windows shaded with cherry wood Venetian blinds. An LCD projector hung from the ceiling, and data ports were available for accessing the Department of Security network around the table.

"Please have a seat, Director DeSouza," Dalembert said, breaking the silence. DeSouza obeyed, taking the vacant seat nearest to where he stood.

"Thank you, DeSouza. You will be an integral part of this operation," Dalembert hissed sarcastically.

DeSouza, not wanting to sound weak, responded, "In what capacity, Sir? I am far too old and rickety to keep up with the likes of these fine agents."

"Oh, you're quite right, DeSouza. You'll be acting as a special advisor to me on this mission. I want you in the field by my side, advising me on the best course of action and attack while we're inside the city walls. If we move outside of Cincuenta Yuno, you won't be expected to continue on. Your usefulness will have ended. On the inside, I need your street savvy. Most of the agents here do not have street experience," Dalembert explained insensitively.

"I'll be glad to help in whatever capacity I can, sir." The last word left DeSouza's tongue stiffly. Being under Dalembert's command was painful.

"That's wonderful. Well said, *Ex*-Director DeSouza." DeSouza flinched, which seemed to delight Dalembert further.

"The research performed by Agents Kim and Yusuf confirms everything we had seen in DeSouza's presentation. However, it failed to identify the next expected target," Dalembert said. He grabbed a flash disk from his pocket and loaded it in one of the open drives on the table. Dalembert picked up a pointer as the file loaded onscreen. It flashed to life, displaying what seemed to be a blueprint.

"We are looking at a three-dimensional schematic of Cincuenta Yuno. Unknown to most, Cincuenta Yuno is a new city. It was built primarily on top of the desert. More importantly, however, Cincuenta Yuno was built on top of the most important resources of the Unified Americas," Dalembert explained. The schematics that Dalembert referred to depicted a significant structure beneath the city.

"Before the unification of the Americas and subsequent wars with Mutie rebels, this location was a military stronghold. It was referred to as Area 51." Dalembert paused for effect.

Everyone around the room was familiar with the lore of Area 51. Legends of clone testing, alien remains, and bleeding-edge weaponry flashed through the thoughts of the agents. The table sat silently, eyeing each other. Most people dismissed the stories as pre-war fables.

"We think Hector was aware of the existence of Area 51 and had detailed layouts to enable its infiltration and destruction." Dalembert paused. DeSouza took the opportunity to interject.

"Why would Muties care about Area 51? And why would you think Hector had any information pertaining to it? Nothing gathered by our intelligence or interrogation revealed any such information," DeSouza questioned skeptically.

Dalembert chuckled. "Yes, the infamous interrogation techniques of the Department of Sanitation. He *lied*. Hector was being leaked information from the inside. The Department of Security located the traitor from within. They were brought to justice. Sadly, it wasn't before the Department of Sanitation had *interrogated* Hector. We had scheduled the destruction of all of Hector's belongings and property. Still, we again find ourselves cleaning up the Department of Sanitation's mess. We really should consider a name change."

DeSouza was hurt at the harsh words directed at his post and previous life. "That still doesn't explain why the Muties would care about Area 51."

"Yes," Dalembert said coolly, not attempting to hide the hint of impatience in his voice. "Area 51 is an integral outpost to the success of Cincuenta Yuno and the Unified Americas. Sensitive testing is performed within. It holds the key to eliminating Mutie DNA from infecting our offspring. The Mutie vaccine is near. Once vaccinated, we can move to phase two of the operation. An assault on all Mutie-occupied territories. We will eliminate the threat from within, then eliminate the external remnants of the disease. Area 51 still remains a weapons depot for the Unified Americas. Under Mutie control, they could set back the vaccination effort and gain control of significantly more firepower. It could tip the balance."

Agents nodded around the table, including DeSouza, who let the weight of the threat sink in.

"We think the next move of our targets will be to attempt infiltration. We have gathered this team to intercept and capture the two *alive*. If this cannot occur safely, then we are to use lethal force. The primary function of this team is to prevent and detain. The tragedy that befell many of our officers did yield insights. We agree with your hypothesis, DeSouza," Dalembert said, turning to the director.

"Our intelligence indicates that some sort of sound weaponry is the most likely cause of the carnage we witnessed in your presentation. With that in mind, our developers have created a modified polycarbonate armor to withstand such an attack. Their sacrifice will ensure our success and sustain our mission: preserving Norm lives and eliminating the Mutie disease. For now, we will break. We'll meet back here in four hours to receive orders. Is that clear?" Dalembert surveyed the room coolly.

"Are there any questions?" he dared.

The room was silent.

"Good, you are dismissed."

The men rose and began to file out. DeSouza wondered what Dalembert had in mind for him during the upcoming operation. Based on their short interaction, DeSouza was sure it wouldn't be pleasant.

CHAPTER 11

It had been some time since DeSouza had heard the clicks and snaps of heavy artillery being prepared for battle. The meeting room, sparse and empty just four hours prior, was littered with body armor, artillery, and sewer schematics. The black suits had been discarded for less formal attire. The dressing down affected the mood of the room. Agents joked with each other as they prepared for battle. It transported DeSouza to when he was a young officer.

He was greeted by agents Luis and Foglia. The agents, wired for the upcoming battle, tried to bring their old boss into their conversation. DeSouza, still lost in the chaos of recent events, grunted when he perceived a response was expected from him. His mind was still racing. Just hours ago, he was Director of the Department of Sanitation. He was in control. Cincuenta Yuno was safe. Officers were alive. He reeled from how quickly his reality had slipped away. The weight of the day sank in as the incident's shock began to wane.

DeSouza watched as the agents browsed through the racks of weaponry, inspecting the chambers and loading and ejecting ammunition cartridges. Most of the weaponry on display was unfamiliar to him. He was only accustomed to standard Department of Sanitation issue. These weapons were a different breed.

"Sir — sir, are you alright?" Luis asked, noticing DeSouza's absent stare.

A smile came over DeSouza's face as he responded to his prodigy from many years ago. "Luis, you're not my direct report anymore. You can drop the 'sir' bit."

"Sorry, sir — I mean, DeSouza. Force of habit, y'know? Are you alright?" Luis continued, a hint of his Caribbean ancestry clinging to his words.

"Yes, Luis, I'm fine. I've never seen any of this gear before. I was just admiring everything. Taking it all in."

"Yes, si — DeSouza, we won't have to deal with those hand-me-downs that the Department of Sanitation was accustomed to all those years ago. These are top-of-the-line. You want to go shopping?"

DeSouza chuckled at Luis' enthusiasm. "Sure, show me what you got."

Luis rose and motioned DeSouza to follow him. The once-silent, elegant, wood-trimmed room had lost its austerity to a barracks' metallic coolness. They made their way past Agent Tarrick, who was armoring up and loading his weaponry of choice.

The sturdy Tarrick selected dual turbines that could deliver a hundred rounds per second. The turbines were heavy and cumbersome, typically mounted on vehicles, but Tarrick had the frame to carry them. They attached under his hulking forearms, powered with an air compression unit strapped on his back. The turbines had a quick release so Tarrick could shed the massive artillery once his ammunition had been spent.

DeSouza and Luis edged around the broad agent to make their way to the weapons table.

"Have you thought about what kind of gear you want?" Luis asked.

"No, I'm not even sure what I'm looking at."

Luis smiled. "Well, what kind of attributes are you looking for?"

"I'm an old man, not like you young bucks. I'll need something lightweight that doesn't have a lot of action."

Luis paused in contemplation. "I think we have just the thing."

DeSouza followed Luis to the end of the table, passing Agents Yusuf and Thompson, who were engaged in an argument about the best blend of weaponry for the mission. Luis picked up a small hybrid. He inspected it and handed it to DeSouza. Accepting the curious weapon with a brief inspection, he looked to Luis for an explanation. The gun was double-barreled but had a pistol's handle, trigger, and sights. It was reasonably light, but DeSouza was concerned about the action. Anything double-barreled usually meant there was some kind of kick.

"The shaft is shock-absorbing if that's what you're worried about," Luis remarked, sensing DeSouza's uncertainty.

Luis continued. "It's made of fiberglass, which is why it's so light. You won't feel a thing. It's quick-loading and has a wide spray. If you're pointing it at something, you'll probably hit it."

DeSouza inspected the firearm, impressed. "I'll take it. Do you have it in a midnight gray?"

Luis smiled. "You want one or two? One for each hand?" he asked.

"No, I'd like to have the other hand free. I would like a backup, though. Do you have any of those Department of Sanitation pea shooters I grew up on? I'll want something familiar just in case."

Luis' smile broadened. "I'm sure I can scrounge one up for you."

"Agents, front and center!" Dalembert's voice rang out through the room.

Luis and DeSouza stiffened at the command. They moved into position. The lights dimmed, and the LCD projector flickered. The wall lit up with a layout of the entrance to Area 51.

"Alright, everyone, Agent Kim has devised a strategy. Onscreen, you are looking at the only accessible entrance to Area 51 in the sewer network. Agent Kim has devised a plan to ensure we are in a position to surprise the enemy. In preparation, we've deployed perimeter drones to scan and alert in the case of a breach."

DeSouza could see the names of the agents positioned on the schematic. "Each of you sees your position? We will be deployed in heat and sensory-deprived pods. They're linked to the perimeter drones. An open com link will be established between the pods to launch our assault. The pods will prevent sound wave attacks in case the enemy performs a sweep before their assault. They will provide the element of surprise and prevent detection from any sensory equipment the enemy may have. On my mark, we will emerge and take the targets down. I want to remind you that we've been ordered to use lethal force only if necessary. This is a capture mission."

At the last comment, a murmur spread across the room. DeSouza suspected the targets would not survive.

"Now, as you can see, we are not using standard-issue headgear. The headshell will mitigate the sound wave weaponry that was used previously. However, as you see, it is a clear bubble. It *does not* offer the same protection against artillery. After conducting the postmortem of the Helena's Tavern site, it was concluded that there was no evidence of projectile weaponry used by the enemy. But it's important to note that not all of the weaponry was recovered. It is safe to assume that the enemy has now acquired firepower. As we know, the only weaponry utilized in the assault was passive. The headshell should be sufficient. But I want you all to be aware, so you can act accordingly. If the weapons we have here fall into the hands of our targets, the shell will not provide sufficient protection. Don't let that happen!" Dalembert's eyes were fixed on DeSouza. DeSouza felt his face flush.

"The armor we are using should be more familiar to most. DeSouza, this is outside the standard issue of the Department of Sanitation but similar in composition. It will prevent most piercing attacks, but a strategically placed hit could kill from impact. Some intelligence shows that Muties have demonstrated this ability. Be sure to avoid close contact and exposing any vitals."

Bathed in light again, Dalembert made his way around the room with agent Kim. Both were already suited in armor, ready for battle with diamondback auto rifles. DeSouza was familiar with the weapon. He was waiting for the Department of Sanitation to be given the issue after the Department of Security field tests. The long rifle fired rapid bursts of either passive or aggressive ammunition. The rifle barrel was shaped like a diamond to quickly load and eject casings in a single action. It could clip on an officer in various fashions, on the arm, the leg, or in the hands, and the trigger could be separated from the grip and held in the palm of one's hand. Dalembert and Kim handed out the bubble-like head shells that would protect the unit from sound-wave weaponry.

DeSouza didn't feel very useful. The controller told him he would be a *special advisor* because of his street knowledge. But the strategy was set without his input. Looking at the map, noting his assigned position, he felt like cannon fodder. Front of the line, first to feel the power of the enemy defenses. DeSouza wasn't the type to complain. He was happy for the opportunity to avenge the lives of his officers. Whether dead or alive, it was a good legacy to leave. If he lived, he might be able to stay on the force in some capacity. Dalembert made his way to DeSouza and personally handed him the headshell.

"Listen, DeSouza, I want you to lay low and stay out of the way. These soldiers are the best of the best. Let them do what they've been trained to do. You've already been the cause of one failure. I don't want you to be the cause of another one," Dalembert said, staring coldly into DeSouza's eyes.

Refraining himself from saying something unprofessional, DeSouza seethed. He was neither cannon fodder nor scenery. But DeSouza knew it was essential to respect the chain of command.

"Understood, sir," he replied curtly.

"Good. The only reason you're here is because of Controller St. Jean. I don't disobey orders. I hope you don't either." Dalembert forcefully handed over the head shell and moved on.

Luis, having heard the exchange, spoke in a hushed voice. "Don't listen to him. He doesn't know you like Foglia and me."

DeSouza turned to Luis. "Hey, I've been in his situation before. I never liked going in with an unknown. I'm an unknown to him, and he doesn't like it. His hand has been forced, and it makes him uncomfortable. I would've felt the same way,"

"Still," Luis replied, "there's no need to talk to anyone that way."

The two stood silent as Dalembert and Kim finished handing out the head shells. Dalembert turned to the unit. "Alright, team, prepare to move out. You have fifteen minutes to finish suiting up and arming yourselves. Remember what's at stake here — the potential future of the Norm race, your children, your friends, and your family. I want everyone on high alert and to follow orders. Do not act until you hear my mark. Is everything understood?"

"*YES, SIR!*" was the unified response.

"Good. Now, before we leave here, Agent Kim will debrief you on your positioning. Make sure you check in with him. We move in fifteen."

DeSouza began suiting up. Luis had found him a standard-issue department pistol, as promised. DeSouza tucked it away in his armor, thanking the friendly face. DeSouza watched the team get ready. The twins, Dean and Palmer, checked each other's armor and weaponry as they suited up. Franklin and Yusuf, their argument long over, were also assisting each other. Tarrick sat alone, slapping his clenched jaw, psyching himself up for the pending action. DeSouza let Luis check his armor but refused the responsibility of doing the same. Foglia assisted his long-time friend instead. The three made their way toward Agent Kim for debriefing.

CHAPTER 12

"Well, what do we have here?" Ari said enthusiastically. She spread out the information from Hector's office. Ari noticed a key fob along with blueprints of some sort of compound among the tubes and folders. Ari could feel Helia's warm breath as she leaned into Ari's body to share the halogen lantern's light. Her eyes darted, taking in all the information. Ari caught herself studying Helia more than the blueprints. Helia, feeling her stare, looked at Ari and smiled. Ari flushed bashfully, ashamed of her overtness.

"So, do you have everything in front of us memorized with that eidetic memory of yours?"

"Hey! You finally got eidetic right." Helia winked.

"It's funny — you don't look any different when you memorize things like that. But the gears are clearly turning up there," Ari explained aloud, trying to make her staring at Helia seem like a scientific endeavor.

"Maybe not, and maybe nothing *is* different. It just sticks for me," Helia replied matter-of-factly.

"What do you make of this?" Ari asked, trying to steer the conversation away from her interest in Helia.

"The depth markings lead me to believe this is an underground structure." Helia rustled through the papers and began to speak almost to herself. "Yes, this looks like a munitions depot, where artillery is stored. There are a bank of workstations. Here, I think we have a weapons testing laboratory — " Helia gasped and stopped suddenly.

"What is it?" Ari asked.

"It looks like some sort of genetic factory based on these annotations," Helia mumbled. Ari didn't find the realization helpful. Helia became distracted and started rustling through the papers. She frantically consumed everything she could.

She whipped through page after page. Ari shifted uncomfortably in the silence. The light of the halogen lamp showed Helia becoming paler with each page.

"What is it?" Ari pleaded.

Helia finished rifling through the information, grabbed the key fob, and looked at Ari.

"They've been experimenting," Helia said. "Hector's intelligence indicated that the Norms have been cloning Mutant DNA to create super soldiers to fight for them. It wasn't successful. The papers described uncontrollable behavior. So, they used the clones to experiment on Mutant abilities, looking for weaknesses. It seems that they've shifted their efforts to develop a vaccine. They're looking to eliminate the strand of DNA that carries the Mutant genes. The trials were successful on clones. They're now experimenting on...." Helia's voice trailed. She shook herself. "They've been stealing people from the Freelands!" Helia rifled through more papers, quickly scanning them. "They're developing some kind of genetic weapon that could be used to commit genocide on Mutants. It would be harmless to Norms, but Mules...." Helia's voice trailed off.

"What about Mules?" Ari asked.

Helia shook her head. "Ari, you all have Mutant DNA, too. It would kill us both." Helia paused, and they both sat in silence.

Helia continued. "The strategy is to incapacitate this outpost. It would lower Cincuenta Yuno's defenses, allowing a Freeland invasion to eliminate progress on a Mutant antigen."

Helia looked at the key fob in her hand. It contained a virus that would destroy all the data collected from the experiments. Holding the device up, Helia explained.

"This is the key. It will destroy all their work and infect their network. The map shows a single Cincuenta Yuno access point. There is a card pass and a combination sequence that Hector had stored. He also has an iris simulator to get past the scanning device. The entrance is in the sewers. I don't remember seeing this location on the map you drew. Do you know where this is?"

Ari looked over the blueprints.

"Yes, I know where that is."

"Can you get me there?" Helia asked.

"Of course."

"Good, we should get on the move."

"Okay, but — "

"No buts — the quicker we strike, the less likely they will be prepared for us."

"You said that last time."

"True, and we're still alive."

"True," Ari responded hesitantly. She knew they were destined to make their way to the entrance site regardless of her objections.

"Let's get ready to move out!" Helia said triumphantly.

Ari moped. She helped Helia pack up the information they had scattered across the floor. She looked over the edge and into the darkness of the sewers. She could hear the rushing flow of sludge making its way through the veins of Cincuenta Yuno. On the landing, Ari felt safe. No one could approach them without being seen, below or above. She knew they had to act, but Ari would rather find safety and hide. Ari couldn't understand Helia's enthusiasm to jump into danger. She would never willingly jump into danger — at least, not before she had met Helia. Ari did admire Helia's ability to take action nonetheless. She always had to be in motion. Ari wondered what Helia would be like without a mission. Could she just sit at the pub? Ari couldn't imagine it, which made it difficult to imagine them together beyond their mission. Ari sighed. There may not be a future beyond their mission, anyway. Regardless of what happened back at Helena's, their survival did not seem likely.

Ari looked at Helia. She was falling for her. Her soft, delicate features, her mysterious abilities, her mission. Helia was a hero. It had stirred something in Ari, given her hope, a purpose. That inspiration was because Helia needed Ari, which might have made her a hero too. Still, neither was something Ari was used to. She thought she might just be mesmerized by the unfamiliar territory. She had never felt the same about anyone else. Ari thought that maybe she had just never been around another person like Helia. There had been opportunities, Mule and Norm women alike. But Ari felt that she would never find happiness in a partner. Maybe it was the drinking or the reason she turned to drink. It wasn't conscious. Something had happened over time. Ari couldn't find happiness in work, love, or friendship, so she found it at the bottom of a bottle. It dulled her hate and anesthetized her to her loneliness. Drinking was the only thing Ari was willing to commit to. It gave her peace and asked for nothing in return. But since meeting Helia, Ari didn't miss the drinking. She felt alive in a new way. It was a rebirth. She knew she'd do anything for Helia. Helia didn't even need to ask. There was a rewarding satisfaction in being needed by someone she admired.

"Pick it up, Ari. We need to move out," Helia said, breaking Ari's trance. "Any minute wasted is a minute that we're giving the department to mobilize. I don't want to give them anything, do you?"

Ari smiled. If it had been just twenty-four hours ago, someone talking to her that way would get a taste of her fist. But a day changed everything. Ari knew taking control was deeply ingrained in Helia's nature, and serving that nature was Ari's privilege.

"Alright," Ari replied, "if you're bent on committing suicide, fine. Let's make it worth it!"

***

Helia frowned. She could feel that Ari was torn. She remembered feeling her pain back at her apartment. It was a cloud that hovered over Ari. Helia was empathetic. Ari might not know it, but Helia admired her. Ari was her hero — she saved her life. She was risking her own life for Helia for no other reason than to avenge the memory of a close friend. That type of loyalty was the sign of a special person. Helia knew that Ari couldn't see herself in that same light. Helia felt a pang of guilt at the feelings stirring within her. She worried she didn't have the same loyalty — too quick to forget Emily and her life before the mission, before Troy.

Ari was the only person she knew who lived day-to-day in Cincuenta Yuno. Helia's mother was from Cincuenta Yuno but escaped after learning she was pregnant with a Mutant child. It was how Helia came to be a Freeborn. Helia's mother often told her stories about Cincuenta Yuno. That was many years ago, though. The stories felt distant — out of date. Even at the time, they seemed fantastic. Her mother spoke of her past enthusiastically. The past brought a twinkle to her eyes.

When she was young, Helia believed that Cincuenta Yuno was where she wanted to live. The only time Helia's mother became somber about the past was when Helia asked about her father. It was apparent that whatever had happened to him was a source of great pain. When she was old enough, her mother informed her that Norms had killed Helia's father because of her escape from Cincuenta Yuno. It was that moment that changed Cincuenta Yuno for Helia's mother.

Outside of her mother, Ari was the only person she knew who was connected to Cincuenta Yuno. That connection quickly bonded her to Ari. Helia was familiar with the history older Freelanders had taught her. Still, it all seemed like a surreal dream. Ari was real and had survived years of oppression in Cincuenta Yuno. She admired her perseverance. There was a wisdom and strength that Ari carried with her, even though she might not know it.

Since the raid, Helia couldn't pick up anything from Ari. Helia, a natural empath, found it disconcerting that she couldn't read Ari. Maybe it was the stench of the sewer or being drained from the matter blast. Helia had never unleashed her power to that degree. She was in unchartered territory and didn't know if this was a side effect. Helia felt her anxiety grow. She had to attempt to read awkward facial expressions and body language. Helia had noticed a change in Ari since they left the apartment. The slouched shoulders and air of despair that enshrouded had begun to slowly lift. She was moving with more purpose. Helia worried that her soldier instincts may have been too harsh for Ari. She didn't want to feel like an oppressive force, like the one that burdened Ari her entire life.

"Ari, you've done more for me than I could have ever asked," Helia began. "Out in the Freelands, we're a unit, bound together for survival. We need to protect each other. But you're not even a member of my clan, and you've risked everything to help me. I'd be dead already if it wasn't for you, and nothing I can say could express my appreciation." Helia paused. She could tell that her words had an impact.

"But when it comes to warfare, I can't help but lead, take control of the situation. I am a soldier, and soldiers give orders. I have been trained my entire life to perform this task. If I fail, my life is for nothing. That's why I risk it so easily. I can't ask the same of you. So, if you feel you can't do this at any time, you shouldn't. Please don't feel obligated to stick by me. You have no obligation to risk your life too. But if you choose to stay, I ask that you follow my judgment. I know that some of my ideas are risky, but this entire mission is risky. I'm a Freeland infiltrator in a Norm compound, and if I'm caught, it will cost me my life. This won't be easy. So, although I may seem abrupt, I don't want you to feel that I am abusing your kindness. I don't have that right."

Helia ended her speech and watched Ari. Ari stiffened. Her jaw clenched, and her eyes glistened as she met Helia's.

***

Ari had never been spoken to in such a way. She had never been appreciated. Ari already knew she couldn't leave her. Helia just gave her another reason to stay without even realizing it. It was a foreign sensation to be appreciated. Ari had never felt the stirring in the pit of her stomach she felt at that moment. Ari felt her emotions swell. She clenched her jaw to prevent the weakness from overwhelming her.

The two stood silent — in a sort of limbo, perfectly still, between the rush of the sewers and the surface above them. Helia stood in front of her waiting for a sign. Ari was motionless, trying to master herself. Ari broke the silence.

"Well, you heard the lady," Ari said to a mock audience. "Time to move. What are we waiting for? We're giving the enemy the upper hand. They already have numbers on us. They don't need time, too," Ari said with a playful wink. A tear escaped her closed eye, making its way down her cheek.

Helia smiled and hugged her. Ari stiffened further at the show of affection and physical contact. Helia's warm breath vibrated in Ari's ear.

"Thank you," Helia whispered.

Ari felt Helia's full lips tickle her ear. Ari felt more tears escape. She smiled and whispered, "C'mon, let's move."

Helia looked down at her. Their faces were close enough that Ari could almost kiss her. She looked away, afraid that her eyes might expose how she really felt

"We will, as soon as *you* finish gathering our supplies," Helia said through a smile also stained with tears.

Helia held Ari's gaze. Their physical proximity seemed natural. Helia seemed to have no reservations about being so close to Ari. Ari, not as comfortable with open expressions of emotions, struggled.

Ari broke the trance. "Two sets of hands get us out of here faster than one."

"*Alright*," Helia responded. "I'll help you pack us up, and we'll move out."

"Yes, sir!" Ari motioned a mock salute, hoping her attempt at humor would hide the deeper emotions she was feeling.

Helia smiled. They packed their weapons, information, and supplies. They had considerable loot from their assault on the Department of Sanitation. Helia still possessed her zip gun and hunting knife. In addition to her body armor, Ari had stolen several automatic weapons loaded with rubber bullets. They organized the information taken from Helena's Tavern. Helia made sure specific papers were stored more accessible. After they finished, they surveyed the area one more time, turned their backs, and made their way to the outpost.

CHAPTER 13

DeSouza was restless. Sitting in stasis, awaiting a perimeter alarm to sound, was not part of his DNA. It took him back to his early days on the force when he would participate in stakeouts. He hated them. DeSouza preferred action. Dalembert had placed him at the front line. The "advisor" had become a human shield. Luis and Foglia objected and volunteered to take DeSouza's place. DeSouza, touched by the loyalty that still coursed through his past officers' veins, refused. DeSouza was proud; he didn't want special treatment. He didn't want to be a liability. It had been many years, but DeSouza had been in this position before — not having the respect of his leader. It was up to him to prove his worth. DeSouza looked at the situation as an opportunity for redemption. Redemption for his reputation and the lives lost under his watch.

The lost souls haunted him. They infected him to the point of blood lust. His inner fire burned out of control, but he didn't let it boil to the surface. He remained calm and obedient, relishing the opportunity for revenge. He wasn't upset about being placed at the front line. He welcomed it. He'd get the first crack at the Mule and the Mutie scum.

The strategic position of the unit had Luis and Foglia ready to provide DeSouza with support. Luis and Foglia pleaded with Dalembert to allow DeSouza to bring up the rear and provide strategic insight to the front lines, but Dalembert didn't want anyone undermining his authority. He was worried that once the artillery started to fly, DeSouza would attempt to take control. With Luis and Foglia obviously loyal to DeSouza, Dalembert didn't want anything to divide his unit's single purpose: to subdue and capture the infiltrators. DeSouza was sympathetic, understanding Dalembert's concern. He would have felt the same way under similar circumstances. Despite Luis and Foglia's objections, he agreed with his leader and took his position on the front lines. It was also a step towards earning back his respect. But it served the desire fueled by his fury. The more he was seen as expendable, the more freedom he had to act.

DeSouza was strapped into the pod. This would help protect him if the enemy used a similar sound wave blast to sweep the area. The straps would prevent him from slamming against the pod walls if it was struck and thrown in an attack. The straps were on a quick-release cord attached to his suit that would safely drop him into the fray. Like all the units, DeSouza's pod was strategically placed above the entrance, anchored to the sewer walls. Dalembert thought the added measure would further protect the team from a potential sweep attack. Dalembert assumed the pods and headgear would protect the unit, but he wasn't positive. Once the perimeter was breached, silent alarms would flash within the pod. When the trespassers crossed the perimeter, the pods would release the soldiers so they could attack from above. Dalembert thought this would also provide the additional strategic advantage of surprise. DeSouza admired the strategy. Under different circumstances, he felt he and Dalembert could be a good team.

The smooth, curved concrete walls engulfed the Area 51 entrance. The pods didn't release any body heat, sound, or light. They ran silently on a small hydrogen cell that was invisible to most detection devices. The pods were all equipped with one-way intercoms that Dalembert controlled. The soldiers could only be given orders, not respond. DeSouza understood the need for control. The team was brought together quickly without enough time to bond and work as a unit. The control over communications would ensure that the team focused on their abilities and what was in front of them, avoiding the hesitation that can occur when too many voices try to talk at once.

DeSouza, strapped to the pod, was immersed in darkness. The stillness left him alone with only his memories, imagination, and anticipation to pass the time. He reflected. He knew his presence on the mission was foolish. He could feel the polycarbonate armor conflicting with his old body. It had been decades since DeSouza was fully armored. The stiff polycarbonate armor struggled to mold him back into a young, muscular soldier. He wondered how Harris had ever been able to manage.

He knew the mission was suicide for him. DeSouza didn't think he had much to risk. He had lost his wife and unborn child years ago. Now, he had lost his job. There wasn't much left. There was only revenge. Maybe if DeSouza was a young man, he could look at the demotion as a challenge to rise back in the department's ranks and the eyes of his peers. Too old, DeSouza wasn't up for the climb. His thoughts turned to his wife. He knew she wouldn't let him take such a pessimistic stance on his prospects. DeSouza missed her greatly, and he missed the family they could have been even more.

DeSouza remembered kissing his wife's swollen belly before they *knew*. He often wondered who their child would be if they had lived. What *their* life would have been. DeSouza imagined their unborn child. Would they have taken to studies? Would they love athletics? Would they enter the force like DeSouza? He sighed. If alive, their child would be nearing twenty. Their adult life just starting. DeSouza often smiled at the thought that, in some parallel existence, he could soon be a grandfather.

With nothing but the darkness, the thought spread. An alternate reality where DeSouza had everything that he'd lost. He poured himself into the younger officers when he first lost Donna and their child. DeSouza found joy in his fatherly relationship with his officers, but it couldn't fully replace the void. Eventually, all his prodigies left. They would start their own families and further their careers. Maintaining contact was difficult when people were pulled in different directions. They would all leave. DeSouza would inevitably find himself alone. There would still be a bond between DeSouza and his prodigies — Luis and Foglia were evidence of that — nevertheless, DeSouza was alone. He was alone at the office. He was alone when he left the office. Now, he was alone in the pod.

If he had a family, DeSouza would never be alone. He could have failed at work and lost his job, but he would still have his family. As time passed, that had more value. DeSouza would trade all his success to find a crack in the space-time continuum. One that would enable him to escape to an alternate universe where he could be with them. DeSouza could handle anything else.

The unforgiving silence of the pod gave no solace. His mind raced. His heavy breathing grew, echoing throughout the pod. DeSouza could feel the walls close in on him. He strained to hear beyond the pod, but his ears were filled with the sound of his pounding heart. Deafened, DeSouza struggled to breathe. His eyes darted, searching the surface of the dark pod for a sign. It was empty. He was a prisoner in the darkness.

DeSouza had lost control. Everything that he had just hours prior was gone. At some level, he was aware that he was letting circumstances have their way with him. But he did not have the strength to fight the demons that haunted him.

Imprisoned in the pod, his imagination raced. *What if I was abandoned? What if this is Dalembert's plan to get rid of me?* DeSouza thought he heard whispers. Whispers of the dead officers, cursing him for sending them to their doom. Donna shook her head in shame. The sweat of his brow stung his eyes with salty fire. DeSouza opened his mouth to scream.

The alarm sounded.

The perimeter had been breached. The wall of DeSouza's pod lit up with two objects. It was the Mutant and the Mule. Each was represented by a red dot. The surface of DeSouza's pod acted as a screen. It lit up in a grid of the area surrounding the entrance to Area 51. Each soldier in the unit was represented by a blue dot.

He shook his head, trying to regain focus. The one-way intercom crackled with Dalembert's voice. "The prey has entered the perimeter."

"DeSouza, Tarrick, Dean, and Palmer, you will be the first wave. You will be released as soon as the infiltrators enter grid areas H5 to H12. Keep an eye on their position and prepare yourselves."

DeSouza watched the two red dots dance closer toward the center of the grid. They fluttered like flies caught in the trance of a lamp light. His heart beat heavily in anticipation.

"C'mon, c'mon," DeSouza pleaded to the two red dots on the wall of his pod. "Just a little closer, and — "

The hatch of the pod opened and released DeSouza. The flash of artificial light and the noxious air of the sewers assaulted his senses. He plunged below, ready for battle.

CHAPTER 14

Helia crept through the tunnels of the Cincuenta Yuno. She was on high alert. The loss of some of her abilities left her blind to detecting any Norm threats. Enemies could be hiding, ready to pounce on the two, and she would be none the wiser. Under normal circumstances, she could move confidently, knowing that her senses would tip her off if danger neared. The sewage coursing through the tunnels was ankle-deep. She could feel it ooze around her legs as she moved forward. Helia's muscle control was cat-like, moving forward without making a sound. Helia hugged the walls and listened for any sign of a potential ambush.

Ari could have been stealthier. She sloshed through the sewage like she was a child playing in puddles. It wasn't her fault. She didn't notice until Helia couldn't stand it any longer.

"*Shhh*! Try to move quieter. We don't want to announce our presence," Helia hissed.

Ari stopped dead in her tracks. Realizing that Helia was right, Ari began to control her steps. They were quieter but not silent. Ari could sense Helia's frustration.

"It's the best I can do!" Ari pleaded in a whisper.

Helia nodded, but her lips twitched in irritation. Ari's noisy walk was deafening to Helia. It polluted the sewer's air with sound. She strained to hear above it but couldn't tune it out. Helia searched the landscape. There would be no possible way they could be attacked by surprise. The curving walls of the sewers didn't allow for any concealment. The concrete was littered with graffiti tags that read slogans like "Mules Rule" and "Sanitation Equals Incarceration." Voices that needed to speak but were too afraid to be heard. The sewage rushing between their feet wasn't deep enough to submerge an entire body. The tunnels didn't take sharp turns or have angles for someone to hide behind. Still, Helia was anxious. She couldn't use any of her senses to detect danger: Ari's clumsiness was deafening; the lanterns prevented Helia's eyes from fully adjusting to the darkness; her nose couldn't distinguish the scent of aggression. Helia found herself focusing on dark spots and shadows, searching for movement. She would shine her lantern at the shadows, cutting through the darkness to hunt down any activity.

***

Ari watched Helia's lantern beam bob and weave. She could sense her anxiousness. Helia was coiled, bound tightly, ready to spring into action. Ari marveled at how easily Helia navigated the dark tunnels. She moved with purpose, each step calculated. Still, Ari noted some unease in her partner. There was something tentative in each step she took. It wasn't from not knowing her way. It was something else. Ari watched Helia try to catch the shadows with her lantern. Ari almost expected to hear Helia exclaim, *"Aha!"* It bothered Ari to see Helia so jumpy. Despite the impossibility of their situation, Ari wanted Helia to feel safe. She would protect her at all costs. A piece of her knew that they would probably not survive their journey, but Helia wouldn't come to any harm in Ari's presence. Ari would die first. It was the first time Ari wasn't afraid.

Ari was no coward. She had been in many fights. She knew what it was like to be beaten. That sort of thing never affected her. But she lived in fear of Norms and the Department of Sanitation. She never would have overtly crossed them. But it was more than an unfair hierarchy. She was fearful of a future she had no control over. Ari was scared that she would die under the thumb of Norms. She was worried that she could never make a difference. That her life was worthless. Her frequent trips to Helena's helped numb the fear, but she was never free from it.

Ari knew that their mission would probably fail. But even if they couldn't make a difference, trying counted more than she could have imagined. The slight chance at success was enough. It gave her hope. Ari thought back to Helena's Tavern. Maybe making a dent in the Norms' stranglehold on Cincuenta Yuno was possible. Ari always wanted to loosen the Norm grip on her life. Since she met Helia, she felt she could breathe. Ari knew that she was falling in love with Helia. Now the only thing Ari was afraid of was letting her down.

***

The two approached an opening, and Helia stopped to assess it. The clearing was illuminated by artificial light, raised slightly, redirecting the sewage. Helia stopped before reaching the edge of the light. She turned off her lantern. She motioned for Ari to do the same. Ari obeyed. Helia strained to see whether there was any movement beyond the tunnel opening. Satisfied, she relied on her other faculties. Helia closed her eyes and listened, trying to detect anything suspicious. Nothing. Helia threw her lantern into the center of the opening. It landed with a hollow clunk.

"What are you doing?" Ari asked just above a whisper. "You threw away your lantern. You're going to need that!"

"Hush!" Helia looked for a reaction. Ari fell silent, watching Helia move. Helia stretched tall, then quickly crouched, trying to get different vantage points. It felt as though Ari was watching a battle ritual. As Helia stood upright, the dance ended. Helia made her way back to Ari and whispered, "Alright, this is it. We've reached our destination. If we're headed into a trap, it's well disguised. Still, the best thing to do is assume we are."

"What do you want me to do?" Ari asked, wanting to be as helpful as possible.

"Get yourself armed and ready for action. I'm going to see if I can bait them out of hiding. At least we'll get a sense of their numbers and capabilities."

"Things don't usually go well for the bait. You sure that's best?" Ari asked, unable to hide her concern.

Helia nodded. "I'm going to breach the perimeter — be ready."

"But what if they capture you before I can help?" Ari asked in a panicked whisper.

"Be armed and ready. If the enemy strikes, open fire."

"But what if I hit you? I'm not an expert here. It's my first day!" Ari pleaded, trying to inject some humor.

Helia returned a smile. "Don't worry, you won't hit me. I'll be quick. The goal is to determine their strength. We'll retreat, if we can, and reassess. Find a weakness, then strike." Helia felt a pang of guilt. She didn't want to lie to Ari but knew what her partner needed to hear.

"That sounds like a better plan."

"On the count of three, I'm going to rush into the opening. You get into position to cover me. Ready?"

Ari armed herself hurriedly. She powered up her weapon and loaded it with a new clip. A green light began to flicker on the rifle's sight.

"Looks like it."

"Alright then. One, two, three."

Helia burst into the opening like a rocket. After three steps, she launched herself into the air. Ari ran into the clearing and planted herself firmly in the center of the sewer tunnel. She scanned for the slightest movement. All she could see was Helia as she contorted in mid-air. Helia flipped backward, landing by Ari's side.

"See anything?"

"No."

Helia squinted into the opening. "The opening is quite large. I couldn't see a ceiling. It was just dark. If we're going to be attacked, it will be from above."

"What should we do?" Ari asked.

Helia surveyed the opening. She pointed to the other side. "That's our destination. We'll zig-zag to the other side. I'll lead. You follow." Helia paused. Ari nodded. "While we're on the move, I want you to spray the ceiling with fire. Be ready to reload when you run dry. The fire has to be non-stop. Is that clear?"

Ari nodded and grabbed some additional rounds. "Ready."

Helia pointed. "We'll rush there. We'll cut back to that point." Ari felt her heart rate quicken. A mix of fear and excitement boiled inside her.

"On three?" Ari asked as calmly as she could fake.

"On three," Helia agreed.

"One, two, three."

Helia dashed to the corner of the opening. Ari followed behind, spraying ammunition in the air. Helia took in as much as possible as she ran through the open space. The walls were smooth, stretching up into the endless darkness. The light was powerful enough to illuminate about a twelve-foot diameter on the ground. The gray walls reflected the light, producing a sickly glow. Helia reached the first point of their rush. She stopped, waiting for Ari to catch up. Ari asn't far behind, spraying the sky. The staccato drum roll of the rubber bullets being released from the barrel of her rifle echoed in the cavernous opening. Helia listened. The sound of the bullets reaching the ceiling gave an indication of their height. Helia estimated the bullets traveled about thirty feet. The ceilings could be as high as forty feet, though. It was enough shadowy space to hide a significant contingent and artillery. Ari finally reached Helia and crouched beside her, breathing heavily.

"Anything?"

"Nothing."

"Ready to make our next dash?"

"Ready when you are," Ari replied between breaths. She reloaded her weapon.

"Alright, again, on three. One, two, three." Helia dashed diagonally to the far side of the wall. Ari followed behind, spraying bullets as she ran. She focused on keeping the weapon aimed above them. Ari didn't want the kick from the rifle to bring her arm down and potentially shoot anywhere else. She watched Helia run. She was much faster than Ari and ran with trained grace. Ari looked up. The bullets that hadn't embedded into the walls began to fall. All she could see was darkness and the deformed remains of rubber bullets raining from above. The air filled with the echo of shots. Helia reached the wall. Watching Ari run toward her, she switched her gaze from Ari to above. Ari joined Helia, crouching beside her.

"This time?"

"Nothing."

"Alright, let me reload." Ari struggled to discard the clip from her rifle. It hit the floor with a clang. She loaded a full clip, which connected with a loud snap. Ari nodded that she was ready.

"Alright, one last time. One, two, three."

Helia dashed towards the other side of the opening. Ari could see her confidence growing in her strides. Ari began to fill with the same enthusiasm. A belief they were going to be successful. Helia could feel the air tickle the minute hairs on the back of her neck, which stood alert, straining to detect any disturbance around her. Helia made it to the other side and watched Ari run toward her. Ari's rifle started to sway as she tired. The black steel glistened in the soft light of the cavernous opening. It vibrated as it burst round after round into the air. Helia watched as the barrel kicked back. Ari's strong shoulders took most of the abuse. Helia admired her strength. Ari was proving to be a quick study for someone who had never been trained as a soldier. Helia didn't know if she could take the same sustained punishment and keep the rifle steadily pointed skyward. The sound of bullets hitting the ceiling above was almost rhythmical.

Thud.

Thud.

Thud.

Clang.

Helia stood erect at the last sound. That clang meant that a bullet hit something hollow. Ari stopped, noticing Helia had gotten to her feet.

"You hit something other than a wall!" Helia yelled.

Ari stopped firing and looked up.

"Hurry!" Helia pleaded.

Ari ran toward Helia. Before she could make it, there was a rush of air from above. From the shift in air pressure, Helia could feel something coming down on top of them. She counted four distinct entities about the size of soldiers.

"They're making their move!" Helia yelled. "Four of them. Back to the wall! Shoot anything that moves!"

Ari hit the nearest wall and looked up. Four fully armored bodies emerged from the darkness. They plunged to the ground with some sort of cord attached to their backs. Ari let loose with her rifle, only to hear it click empty. She rushed to reload. Helia stayed poised, ready to attack. The bodies hit the ground and released their cords. The two were outnumbered. Their backs against the wall.

Helia turned to Ari. "There's four. I'll go left, you take right. Are you ready?"

Ari felt the click of the new clip in her rifle. She nodded.

The six stood motionless. Ari watched. Each side swayed, waiting for the other side to make the first move.

One of the soldiers seemed to break formation, rushing directly toward Ari.

CHAPTER 15

DeSouza felt the wind push against his armored body as he plunged toward the surface. He fell in silence. The sensory deprivation bubble that protected his head made him impervious to any sound outside the transparent dome. The only thing he could hear was his own breath, which quickened as the ground quickly approached.

The cord attached to his back pulled at him as he neared the surface. He could feel the resistance but knew it wasn't enough to ensure a soft landing. DeSouza's feet hit the ground. A sharp pain rushed up his legs. The pain was so great that DeSouza saw stars as he tried to orient himself. He staggered. He caught his balance, trying to shake off the stars and focus. Everything was blurry. He could make out five bodies but couldn't determine their identity.

DeSouza's eyes searched the silhouettes, trying to penetrate the haze. Watching the stationary bodies, he began to panic. He started to breathe heavier. Even in his silence, he could feel the tension build. It felt like the shadows were watching DeSouza, waiting for him to make the first move. In his panic, he couldn't remember any of the other soldiers' positions. He couldn't remember his orders. He was a complete blank, impotent from his panic.

He gave his head another shake. He wasn't a rookie. He concentrated on measuring his breath. No movement meant he didn't have to make a hasty decision. DeSouza began to recognize details as the haze cleared. He focused on the nearest body — a sturdy, stocky form wearing a black polycarbonate chest plate. It looked familiar. He noticed the Department of Sanitation emblem on the chest. His panic began to return. He wasn't sure he could trust what he was seeing. Unsure if what stood before him was a hallucination. He squinted, trying to make out the lettering on the badge. Slowly, the letters came into focus: H-A-R-R-I-S. DeSouza gasped. His face flushed. He could feel his blood afire with rage. He let out a primal scream.

DeSouza rushed toward his foe, consumed with rage, the armor of his fallen officer taunting him. He embraced his blood lust. His ears rang from the deafening cry that endlessly echoed in his helmet. His prey froze. It was caught in his glare. DeSouza's peripheral vision saw the other bodies flinching at his sudden movement. He ignored their reaction and closed in on his victim. He dropped his weapon as he ran toward the offender of the dead. All rational thought had left DeSouza. He leaped at his target as soon as he was in striking distance and screamed again.

He had become a hunter. He was no longer a trained soldier. As he lunged, he watched his prey struggle with its weapon. He could feel triumph within his grasp. In desperation, it threw a wild punch in DeSouza's direction. He helplessly watched his enemy's fist shatter the sensory deprivation shield. Sound flooded DeSouza's ears. He heard rapid-fire artillery echoing throughout the cavernous opening. In an instant, the realization of his actions struck him.

What have I done? was DeSouza's last thought before his enemy's fist connected with him. The fist collided with DeSouza's jaw. He was instantly knocked unconscious. The force of the punch flung his body against a wall, and he slid to the ground.

***

Ari watched a crazed soldier scramble toward her. It dropped its gun, and its limbs flailed. Ari struggled with her weapon. She tried to raise it and fire, but rapid clicking noises indicated a jam. Ari tried to release the clip, but her foe was too close. She could see the soldier's old and weathered face. His eyes were wild yet vacant. His mouth was agape with saliva foaming at each side, rabid. Ari knew she was not dealing with a sane man.

Ari looked at Helia. She had already leaped away, engaging with the other soldiers. Ari saw her twist in the air and watched the other soldiers fire wildly at her. Ari was alone. If she was going to help Helia, she had to dispose of her threat quickly. The crazed soldier launched at her, trying to tackle Ari. The chaos around her fell away. She did what came naturally and protected herself.

Discarding her weapon, Ari reared back and unloaded a punch at her attacker's head with all the force she could muster. Ari burst through the transparent bubble that enshrouded his enemy's head. She felt the substance crumble feebly against her fist, then felt a shock of pain as her fist connected with the soldier's face. The force of her punch redirected his momentum into the wall beside them. She watched his body go limp. Looking at her victim in a collapsed heap, Ari thought she might have killed the man.

Ari's attention quickly shifted to sharp drumming against her chest. Staggering, she found the source of the attack — a soldier brandishing a spinning turbine in each hand. As the turbines spun, they released a wave of bullets. Ari staggered back at the force of the onslaught, but she regained her balance and stood to meet the artillery. Her assailant stood astonished. The drumming ceased, and Ari watched the turbines spin harmlessly to a stop.

Most people wouldn't survive such an attack. Even if the bullets had not pierced the strong polycarbonate chest plate, the shock of impact would have been enough to kill. Ari's strong Mule form was resilient. She winced at the pain in her chest, but she could stomach pain. She rose and stared triumphantly at her assailant, daring him to try again.

***

Agent Tarrick was in shock. He had never seen someone withstand a barrage of bullets. The tight-lipped smile had been wiped from his face. He thought that he had neutralized one of the targets. He watched it stagger. Tarrick felt his heart begin to race as his enemy regained its balance and defiantly stood its ground. Tarrick released his grip on his turbines. He depressed the quick release, discarding the cumbersome weapons. Tarrick's smile returned. *Finally, a worthy opponent.* Like DeSouza, Tarrick began to rush towards his enemy. Tarrick would take his opponent down with his fists and match strength against strength.

***

Since DeSouza had broken formation, the battlefield had spun into chaos. Dalembert watched the scene from his pod with his mouth agape. He cursed DeSouza. As soon as he broke formation, Dalembert knew it would lead to disaster. He clenched his fists. *I knew it was a mistake to bring the over-the-hill paper pusher on this op*. Dalembert's mind raced. He thought of alternative battle plans. He had to try to salvage the mission, so he opened the one-way intercom.

"Fall back, front line! We need to regroup!" Dalembert barked.

He watched the scene unfold. Tarrick had taken a page from the book of DeSouza, breaking formation and rushing one of the marks. Dean and Palmer tried unsuccessfully to bring down the other target, which danced elusively from captivity or harm. He knew his words were falling on deaf ears. The battle had begun.

"All right, second line, we drop in on my mark. I want Kim to rendezvous with me in the rear. The rest of you hold formation to contain the two targets. We don't want them escaping. Only make a move on my command. We don't want this mission to spin entirely out of control. All right, one, two, three — " Dalembert depressed the release from his pod. The remaining troops fell from their pods.

***

As Tarrick rushed to meet Ari, he heard some sort of rambling in his ear. It was Dalembert's voice. Something about falling back. Tarrick laughed to himself. *Stupid suit, telling me how to do my job. I'm gonna bring down this freak with my own bare hands.* Tarrick, known for being a loose cannon, had never lost a fellow agent on an op, and he was not about to. Seeing how DeSouza was tossed aside like a ragdoll sent fire through Tarrick's veins. He was going to make sure that his perfect record remained intact.

***

Ari watched the soldier discard the weapons attached to his arm. Like the other soldier, he had a clear bubble that encased his head. Knowing the helmet was not sturdy, Ari sought to reload her rifle. She grabbed the nearby weapon at her feet, removed the clip, and deftly reloaded. She felt the new clip click into place. Ari took aim at the soldier rushing toward her. She squeezed the trigger and pushed back against the rifle's kick. Her arms were still weak from covering Helia. The gun wavered in her hand as it released a wall of rubber bullets. It was her first time shooting at a moving target. As the shots fired from Ari's rifle, her opponent quickly gained ground. She recognized the look of panic and aggression twisting together on the face of her would-be assailant. His strong jaw clenched, and the nostrils on his crooked nose flared. His green eyes glimmered with anticipation through the narrow slits of his eyelids. As he got closer, she could make out tiny freckles that peppered his face. In an instant, the face was obscured by a complex web of cracks that stretched around the orb-like helmet. A bullet from Ari's rifle had pierced the clear bubble. It had been her only direct hit amongst a steady flow of bullets whizzing by their target. She tried to steady her aim, hoping to strike her target again, but the bullets scattered erratically. It was too late. The soldier was on top of her. The shot that pierced his helmet hadn't slowed him. Blinded by the cracked bubble, the soldier reached for Ari. She stepped back and swung her rifle at her attacker's head. She felt the rifle connect with the helmet, which exploded on impact, revealing the soldier's face. The soldier was unfazed. Ari found herself exposed. Still caught in a swinging motion, Ari was twisted, unable to protect herself.

***

Tarrick swore at himself. How could he let his target get armed and fire? His helmet was pierced. The jagged cracks blinded him, and the bullet that passed through allowed the sound from outside to flood his senses. He was disoriented. Tarrick pushed forward, trying to remember his target's position. He grabbed feebly at the air, uncertain, feeling out for where he thought the target might be. Unsuccessful, he felt an impact that pushed at his head. In an instant, the world around him lit. The helmet around his head burst; light pierced his eyes. He noticed that the freak had exposed itself. Its body was contorted from the momentum of its swing. It was helpless. Tarrick struck. He watched the freak's head snap sideways. It staggered back, releasing the weapon.

***

Ari watched helplessly. She clenched her jaw, readying herself for the impact. She felt the sharp strike of the soldier's fist connecting with her jaw, filling her mouth with warm blood. Ari staggered from the blow but quickly steadied herself as she spat a mouthful of blood. The soldier grabbed Ari's neck and punched her again. The fist connected with her nose, making her eyes water and covering her mouth and chin with more red splatter. In desperation, Ari slapped away the soldier's arm from her neck and thrust her head toward the soldier's chin.

***

Tarrick gritted his teeth in a twisted smile. He pounded the freak. Thinking it helpless, Tarrick let his bloodlust possess him. He watched the blood explode from his victim's nose, staining his fist red. It resisted his hold, breaking his grip with a slap. He was surprised at how easily it broke his grip and watched as its large forehead launched at his chin. Tarrick moved his head skyward, trying to avoid impact. He couldn't. Tarrick felt the thick bone of the freak's skull connect with his lower jaw. The force of the blow sent his lower jaw upwards, shattering his gritted teeth. His vision was clouded with stars. He stumbled back, shocked at the force. Tarrick spat out the bloody shards of broken teeth from his mouth. He looked at the freak in astonishment as it regained its footing. Tarrick, infuriated, lunged again.

***

Ari watched the soldier stagger back. Gaining her balance, she taunted him; this had become an old-fashioned bar fight. Familiar territory. The soldier lunged. Stepping aside, she slipped through his attack. Grabbing the soldier's head in her firm grip, Ari planted his face into the ground.

***

Tarrick felt its hand grab his head. He felt it squeeze his temples and watched the ground approach at an alarming rate. He landed with a resounding 'oomph.' The cold ground against his face. Looking up, he saw his opponent's foot. His arm flailed as he tried without success to push it away. There was a pool of bool encircling his head. He realized the danger that he was in. He opened his mouth to curse his foe, but all that came next was a *pop*, and everything went black.

***

Taking advantage of his grounded position, Ari scrambled to her feet. She planted her foot on the soldier's face. He tried to block the impact with his arms, but she quickly grabbed one. Ari looked down at the soldier. He tried to lift his face from the puddle of red to look up at her. A wave of furious realization came over him. He opened his mouth. The final words never came. Ari yanked the soldier's arm, stepping down on the soldier's head with all of her strength. Ari heard a resounding *pop* as she felt the soldier's neck break. Ari watched the body twitch until it went still. She spat out another mouthful of blood.

The noise of battle suddenly engulfed Ari. She had been oblivious, wholly engaged in the melee of her own fight. She took stock of the battle scene. Helia stood over two, muscles shining through the tight, black suit from the fluorescent lighting. Helia turned and met Ari's eyes and began to motion frantically. Ari saw panic in her eyes. She was yelling something. Ari strained to hear her words, but it was too late — everything went black.

***

Helia was in the air as soon as the soldier broke toward Ari. Their comrade's rush froze the other officers. It must not have been part of the plan. Helia knew Ari was safe from being shot at because the soldier would be too close to her for the others to open fire. Helia's leap prompted the remaining officers to wildly fire their weapons at her. She had captured their attention.

Helia felt the bullets zip by her body. She contorted in the air, anticipating the paths of the harmful projectiles. Concentrating, she collected the sound waves that filled the space around her. As she twisted, she thrust her hands toward her assailants, releasing small bursts of sonic blasts. The air bent in front of her, deflecting the bullets but causing no change to the soldiers. Helia's eyes widened, surprised that her blasts had little effect. The soldiers should have been writhing in pain as their eyes and ears burst from her attack.

Her mind raced, trying to determine her next move. It was the first time real fear crept into her mind. Helia felt something slam into her bicep. The pain of the rubber bullet forced a scream out of her. She forced herself to focus. *All right, Helia, time to preserve yourself. They'll make a mistake.* With only one arm available, Helia touched the ground, flipping acrobatically, eluding gunfire.

Helia risked a glance back at Ari. Having disposed of her first attacker, Ari grappled with another. Helia didn't have time to help. She ran up the curved concrete toward the darkness. She felt the bursts of bullets vibrate up her leg as they embedded into the wall behind her. Helia noticed that the bullets whizzing by her had decreased. She angled herself, seeing one of the soldiers turn to Ari. Ari was standing over a dead soldier. Helia launched herself from the wall. She quickly drew her zip gun from her boot clip and fired a single shot. Helia felt the gun kick in her hand. The bullet fled the barrel, piercing a soldier's helmet and entering his eye. Instantly, the clear surface of the helmet was coated in red blood. The soldier collapsed to the ground with a blood-curdling scream. His partner nearby stopped, dropping his weapon and running to his fallen comrade. He removed his helmet and let out a piercing cry.

"*DEAN!*"

***

Palmer raced to his brother. Tears began to stream down his face. Dean was his brother, his partner, and his best friend. The images of their boyhood flashed before his eyes. The small mirror image of himself always by his side and smiling. Palmer couldn't imagine life without him. He watched his brother's body writhe in agony. The fractured helmet was stained with red. Palmer removed it, and blood rushed to the ground, gathering in a thick pool.

Palmer let out a cry. *"NO!"* His shout echoing in his helmet made Palmer realize that his brother couldn't even hear him. He threw it off with no regard for his own safety. "*DEAN!*" he cried.

Oblivious to his surroundings, Palmer cradled his brother and whispered, "It's gonna be alright. It's gonna be alright, it's gonna be alright." He kept repeating the phrase, trying to convince himself. Palmer didn't notice he wasn't alone. He heard a ringing in his ears, and then all went black.

***

Helia watched the soldier rush to the assailant she had just shot. Having removed their helmets, she noticed that they were mirror images of each other. Stealthily approaching, Helia began gathering the chaos into a focused burst of energy. Waving her hand and bending the air in front of her, Helia let forth a sonic burst. The wave passed over the face of the soldier, who was muttering indiscernibly. His eyes burst, and his ears erupted. Blood rushed down his face, replacing the tears. The soldier collapsed over his twin.

She looked up from the deceased enemies to see how Ari was faring. Ari had been staring at her. A moment passed between them. There was only the present as they stood, caught in a vacuum. Helia was the first to break the trance. A shadow licked at the corner of her eye, and her head jerked to notice a soldier creeping behind Ari. She cursed herself. *There must've been more soldiers!* She motioned to Ari. Fear for her partner paralyzed her. She was unable to make a sound. A soldier with a dark complexion and soft features crept behind Ari. His eyes were wide, and his jaw was clenched in anticipation. The soldier drew the butt of his rifle over his head. The look on Helia's face became more frantic. Realization passed over Ari's face. Ari began to turn, but it was too late. The soldier thrust the rifle down between Ari's neck and collarbone. Ari fell to the ground, unconscious. Furious, Helia drew her zip gun into her hand and shot the remaining bullet in one swift motion. She watched as the bullet sliced through the air. The soldier froze, realizing this was his final moment. His eyes widened as the bullet pierced his helmet and embedded itself in his forehead. The soldier stiffened momentarily and collapsed.

Moving towards her fallen ally, Helia heard the thudding of bullets colliding with the wall. She immediately reacted, leaping once again into the air. Her feet touched the wall, elevating her higher to safety. She cursed herself for losing focus. She cursed herself more for allowing Ari to be harmed. Now she had almost let herself get killed. Helia traced the source of the shots. She surveyed her surroundings. Noticing the rifles of fallen soldiers, Helia dove to the surface. Planting her good arm into the ground, Helia kicked up a rifle that lay close by one of the fallen soldiers. The rifle gleamed as it twirled in the air, the light bouncing off the metallic object. She grabbed it as she flipped backward off of the concrete and harnessed the rifle under her arm.

Helia scanned the area to locate any additional soldiers. The gleam of metal in the distance disclosed the location of at least four more. They were spread out, containing her from every angle. Bullets sailed around her as she contorted her body to make herself a harder target. Still bending into impossible shapes, Helia squeezed the trigger of the rifle she held under her arm. The gun jerked, letting forth a burst of artillery. The rifle's kick affected her direction so she allowed the weapon to guide her in the air. She gently pressed the trigger, releasing bursts of artillery in the general direction of the anonymous soldiers. The shots surprised the soldiers. They scattered to regroup.

Helia caught a flash of reflecting light from the corner of her eye. Two soldiers were rushing to converge on Ari. Helia moved to intercept. The soldiers paused, surveying the first body Ari had incapacitated. Helia planted her feet and pushed off to attack. The movement exposed her. The soldiers turned in her direction, but it was too late. Mid-air, Helia kicked both soldiers simultaneously, shattering their helmets. They staggered back, more surprised than affected by Helia's attack. The sewer was silent. The sound of gunfire had stopped. The soldiers at the perimeter did not want to hit their peers with stray fire. Helia could feel the pressure from the soldiers. Ready to engage in close quarters. Confident that they had numbers.

Back on the ground, Helia spun. Her rifle flashed as she fired two rounds that cut through the silence. The shots echoed in the cavernous opening. Frozen in place, the two bullets struck the helmetless soldiers. They both collapsed, dying instantly. The air erupted with gunfire. Helia, drawing attention from Ari, took to the air, surveying the battle. She counted three soldiers. They were close enough that Helia could make out their faces. Landing, Helia's eyes darted, looking for a strategic advantage. She was surrounded. Caught between the soldiers and the smooth concrete, Helia didn't have many options. She drew her knife and began to run toward the wall. She felt the rapid-fire bullets whiz by her. With her knife in hand, she mustered as much force as possible and planted the blade into the wall.

She screamed as she forced the metal into the concrete surface, feeling the muscles in her wounded arm tear. Helia planted her foot on the handle and launched her body high into the cavern, concealing her in the shadows above. The rifle fire became wilder and panicked as the soldiers lost sight of Helia. She could still see her targets from her airborne vantage point. The rifle fire stopped as she landed behind the soldiers. They turned. Helia could see the panic in their eyes. She grabbed the closest soldier, using him as a shield. She raised her rifle and squeezed the trigger. The two in front of her tried to react, but they were exposed and slowed from shock. The bullets shattered their clear helmets. They were no longer a threat.

The soldier in her grips threw an elbow into her stomach and spun to engage Helia. She took the butt of the rifle and shattered the helmet, kicking him away. He looked at his lifeless comrades, enraged. Silence enveloped the soldier, and his rage turned to confusion as the air bent around him. His face warped as the small wave passed over him, streams of blood erupting from his eyes and ears. His scream got louder as the sound returned to normal, writhing in pain as death overtook him.

Helia's victory was short-lived. She felt a sharp pang in her lower back that toppled her. Spinning to look upward, Helia saw a soldier standing above her, pointing a gun at her face. The soldier had small, rodent-like features. His sunken beady eyes flashed with malice. His black hair was slicked. The corners of his thin lips contorted into a smirk below his pointy, upturned nose. Helia saw his finger begin to tense around the trigger.

BANG!

***

Agent Dalembert couldn't believe his eyes. The battlefield had broken into chaos, and he hated chaos. He couldn't stand it when people deviated from the plan — his plan. He expected as much from DeSouza, who he placed at the front line so he could be disposed of quickly. That unfolded according to plan. But everything else? Tarrick's reaction was unanticipated. Tarrick was cool in battle and not prone to panic, but he had disappointed Dalembert. The twins fell too quickly, their bond a weakness that was easily exploited.

The breakdown solidified Dalembert's faithlessness in others. His planning was never at fault. It was people's inability to stick to the plan that caused failure. Dalembert shook his head. He blamed the Controller for assembling a team of agents without his input, with no planning, to address an immediate threat. The best operations were the result of careful planning and team building. Expecting a group of strangers to work as a cohesive unit in a matter of hours screamed disaster. This was not his fault. Dalembert began to bark on his one-way Polycom.

"Yusuf, I want you to get in position behind the Mule. Take it down! Kim, take out the Mutie from long range. Luis, Foglia, Gooding, Franklin, and Thompson form a containment position. We have them pinned down. Let's finish the job! Move it!"

Yusuf crept silently behind the Mule. Using the butt of his rifle, he struck the Mule unconscious. Dalembert watched and smiled. *There we go. Success comes when we stick to a plan.*

"Kim, what are you waiting for? *FIRE!*" Dalembert barked.

Kim was struggling with his high-powered rifle. It had jammed. It was too powerful for its construction, only good at taking down long-range targets, and even then, only when it worked. Still, Dalembert had witnessed these weapons taking down Muties in the desert that were barely visible with binoculars.

Kim mastered the rifle and shot. The Mutie was on the move again. In the instant it took for Dalembert to take his eyes off her, she had already killed Yusuf and averted Kim's shot. Kim looked at Dalembert in disbelief: he never missed. Dalembert scanned the scene. Chaos had broken out again. Luis and Foglia had rushed to the side of their old leader, DeSouza, and were attending to him. Dalembert shook his head. *Idiots.* He couldn't entirely blame them. Once they heard his command to Kim, they likely thought the Mutie takedown was as good as done. Kim's reputation as a marksman was widely known throughout the force. Dalembert watched helplessly as the Mutie made her way toward the two. In the time it would have taken Dalembert to warn them on the Polycom, she shot two quick rounds of bullets through their helmets. In one instant, they were down. Right alongside their fallen former boss.

"What are you waiting for? I want everyone to open fire! Take the Mutie down!"

The perimeter opened fire, but the Mutie danced and contorted out of harm's way as if she knew where the bullets were going. Dalembert could not believe his eyes. How could she know? He was in awe. Even he couldn't have planned for this. She interrupted his amazement with bursts of artillery.

"Alright!" Dalembert screamed, trying to regain order among his troops. "I want everyone moving. Let's keep containment formation. Move in to keep pressure!"

Dalembert's voice woke his remaining troops. They opened fire. They were close to the Mutie. Less than twenty yards away. Kim, Gooding, and Thompson had her pinned against the wall. Passing through the carnage of Yusuf, Foglia, Luis, Tarrick, and DeSouza, Dalembert thought he detected movement. A twitch, maybe. But his attention was quickly taken back to the battle. Things had changed drastically. He watched as the Mutie seemed to fly behind what was left of the unit. She stood right in front of Dalembert, only a few short yards away, but he could not move. He was frozen. Dalembert stood paralyzed as he watched the Mutie tear apart the rest of his unit. The battle had been a failure.

He felt his blood boil with rage, giving him the courage to move again. Rushing forward, Dalembert closed the distance between the two. Channeling all of his anger, he struck the Mutie in the lower back. He had surprised her. Dalembert felt the Mutie collapse as his weight bore down on her. He stood, looming over the Mutie as she fell forward. She rolled onto her back and looked up at him. He took a moment, studying her. This Mutie scum had been his most challenging foe, but she was just a child. Dalembert scoffed. The battle was a failure, but the operation was a success. He felt an element of respect for his enemy. *Too bad I have to waste her*, he thought. In the end, though, he proved superior. A smirk flashed across his face as he squeezed the trigger.

BANG!

***

DeSouza was shaken into consciousness. His head pounded, and his ears rang. He opened his eyes slowly to see Luis staring back at him. A look of relief passed over Luis' face. He was aware of the sound of gunfire all around him. Suddenly, the drumming of gunfire ceased. Everything had grown silent. DeSouza looked around. *Was the battle over? Did we win?* As he craned his neck to see, a blur of motion flew over the top of him. DeSouza lay prone as he watched the Mutie approach Luis and Foglia. He opened his mouth but didn't have time to get a word out. He heard two rapid rounds of bullets make contact and felt a wet spray on his face. Luis and Foglia crumpled next to him. It was their blood he felt. The noise of battle broke out once more. DeSouza was unable to move. Consumed with anger and shame, he lay paralyzed with grief.

Both young agents were close to him, but Luis was his protege. He felt a paternal bond and took pride in his success. He would never forgive himself for Luis' death. DeSouza broke rank and attacked the Mule. It was selfish. He should've acted with more composure. Years ago, the same act in a young Luis would have been met with a harsh scolding. He was a hypocrite. DeSouza felt warm tears wind their way through the creases of his face. He wasn't sure if he could go on. Too many deaths weighed on his conscience. The image of Donna entered his mind. She would have been disappointed. Maybe even disowned him. He couldn't even fathom what his child would have thought of him. The battlefield blurred. DeSouza blinked, trying to regain focus. That was when he saw her. Donna. She was young, just as he remembered her.

The chaos receded into a murmur as Donna's image soaked into DeSouza's consciousness. The realization of what he was seeing snapped him to attention. He ignored the pain and sat up to see whether the appearance of a young Donna was an apparition. Either way, the sight of her was a message. DeSouza scanned the battle, seeing Donna in danger, under fire, sure to be cornered. He looked at the carnage that surrounded him. The carcasses of soldiers lay strewn about the battlefield. DeSouza struggled to hold on to reality, sure he was hallucinating Donna and the dead soldiers around him. Was this some sort of important message to him from beyond the grave?

The sight of Luis' body awoke DeSouza from his trance. The bodies of Tarrick and the Mule were close by, too. This was no hallucination. The wave of guilt returned. *How is this possible?* He watched her dance away from rifle fire as if she already knew its trajectory. *What is going on here?* DeSouza shook his head, trying to shed his confusion. A shadow caught his peripheral vision. It was Dalembert edging his way closer to the battle. DeSouza noticed Dalembert stop, focused on the fighting ahead; he was poised to attack if an opportunity presented itself. DeSouza saw Donna behind the line of soldiers as if she had teleported. Kim, Gooding, and Thompson were frozen in surprise. A moment of stillness passed. DeSouza studied Donna. She was definitely younger than he had ever known her. She seemed taller and was never as athletic as she looked now. DeSouza noticed that her complexion was darker, more like his own.

His observations were drowned out by the rapid fire of Donna's rifle. She had Kim as a human shield, but it didn't matter. Thompson and Gooding went down without retaliation. Kim made an effort to fight her off, joining his comrades on the concrete an instant later. Kim wasn't lucky enough to get a quick bullet. DeSouza's emotions twisted watching Donna cause so much carnage. DeSousa's onslaught of emotion was interrupted by Dalembert bringing Donna down with a kick to her back. He stood over her, brandishing a pistol. DeSouza knew he meant to kill her. His instincts overtook him. DeSouza quietly moved through shadows for a better position behind Dalembert. The peashooter that Luis had given him as a backup was deadly at close range. DeSouza's aim had to be perfect. He placed the pistol between the space where Dalembert's helmet met armor and pulled the trigger.

BANG!

DeSouza knew that shot finalized the life he knew. It ended quickly. In just over a day, he had lost his job, his officers, and what seemed like his sanity. The visage of Donna gave him hope, a purpose beyond his failures. He lost Donna once before. If *this* Donna offered some sort of penance, he couldn't let her be captured or killed before he found out more.

DeSouza fell to his knees behind Dalembert's carcass. Through tear-filled eyes, DeSouza looked at Donna. She was confused. She didn't recognize him.

"Donna?"

Then everything went black.

***

BANG!

Helia winced. She closed her eyes, bracing for death. Instead, she heard a thud. Helia opened her eyes. The soldier standing over her collapsed to the ground. In his place knelt an older man. He looked at her with expectation, his face creased with bewilderment and hope. He was crying.

"Donna?"

Helia's heart leaped into her throat. That was her mother's name. How did this strange man know her mother? But before she could ask, he slumped forward in a heap. Ari stood over him.

***

Controller St. Jean slammed his desk. His bodyguards flinched, worried their boss' wrath would turn on them.

"Failures!"

He watched the screen as the dotted lives of each team member blinked dark into oblivion. The remaining dot was DeSouza. He seemed to have been captured.

"We'll have to arm the AE defense in the outpost." St. Jean knew the infiltrators didn't stand a chance against the artillery in the Area 51 facility. The AE, or Autonomous Extermination defense were intelligent robotics designed to exterminate any living entity within their programmed coordinates. They would seek and destroy anything that escaped once the protocol was enacted. They were designed to contain outbreaks using lethal force.

"Sir, won't that jeopardize the science team?" one of his attachés asked.

"Expendable!" the controller roared.

The guards shifted uncomfortably.

"Should we send a warning Sir?" the attaché asked.

The Controller shook his head. They couldn't risk their communication being intercepted, or the scientists attempting to disarm the AE protocol to save themselves.

"If we don't eliminate the Mutie threat now, we'll be looking at going scorched earth."

The two stood at attention. They knew the protocol if there was an outbreak. All Cincuenta Yuno would be razed. As St. Jean began to enact the AE defense protocol, one of the aides gathered enough courage to inquire. "Um, sir, would you like us to begin evacuation?"

St. Jean's jaw clenched. "Ever hear of going down with the ship, solder?"

The guard nodded and thought of his family.

***

Ari stood over an unconscious the unconscious soldier, staring wild-eyed at Helia. "You okay?"

Helia nodded, confused. She got to her feet. She noticed Ari holding the backpack filled with everything the mission needed.

"What now?"

Helia shook herself. She couldn't stop staring at the agent who called her by her mother's name. She had to refocus.

"Let's get to the outpost." She paused. "Bring him." Helia nodded to the man. Ari looked at her, confused. "He knew an insider. He might be a sympathizer. If he is, we can't leave him behind," Helia explained.

Ari collected the limp soldier and hoisted him over her sturdy shoulder. She handed the backpack to Helia, who ran ahead the short distance to the outpost entrance.

Helia rummaged through the bag for the iris simulator. After some difficulty adjusting to the scanning device, the outpost doors opened. She waved at Ari to hurry. They entered a sturdy metal lift large enough to transport a convoy. Ari made her way to the wall, placing the soldier on the floor. Helia turned to a console and entered the card pass and a combination sequence Hector had left for them. As the doors hummed and slid shut, the elevator car vibrated and began to move. They had started their descent. Ari studied the middle-aged, wrinkled man who was somehow familiar.

"Weird, isn't it?" Helia interrupted as if reading her thoughts.

Ari nodded.

"Why was this agent part of the troupe? He's much older than any of the others. Doesn't look like a soldier."

Helia walked over to him, crouched down, and studied him. His eyelids fluttered. A moment of recognition passed — he smiled. Then he straightened, eyes wide, body alert. He grabbed Helia.

Helia felt an intense wave of emotion wash over her. Her legs weakened.

"Donna!" the man exclaimed desperately.

Ari moved in. Helia raised her hand in a stop motion. In a soft voice, Helia said, "My name isn't Donna."

"Where is she? How do you look like her?" he pleaded.

Helia, trying to manage the onslaught of desperation coming from the agent, attempted to calm him. "Donna isn't here. Who is Donna?"

He was getting frustrated. "She's my wife!"

Helia's knees buckled. She couldn't comprehend what she had just heard.

Ari stood, not knowing what to do.

"Your w-wife?" Helia stammered.

The man still had a hold of Helia and began shaking her. "Yes! What have you done with her?!"

Ari had had enough. She grabbed the confused soldier and separated him from Helia, standing him up against the wall.

Helia regained her footing and stood. She could feel the man was being sincere. What he was saying was true. But what he was saying was also impossible.

"Donna is my mother's name," Helia said barely above a whisper.

The man's face twisted. It was too much for him to comprehend. He stumbled forward, reaching for Helia.

"Alright, nighty night." With a quick and solid strike, Ari knocked him unconscious once again.

The elevator rumbled to a stop.

Helia looked from Ari to the man. "I think that man might be my fath — "

The doors began to slide open.

"No time for that now." Ari nodded to the doors.

"I think we're safe. I don't sense — "

Artillery erupted. Surprised, the two ducked for cover. The elevator echoed with deafening chaos. Helia cursed herself. She began gathering the swirl of chaos into a concentrated blast. Whoever surprised her was going to feel her full wrath.

The doors slowly revealed a bipedal robot with blasters on each side accompanied by a scope. The torso swiveled, scanning the scene, stopping to lock onto Helia's position. Helia rolled across the cold metal floor. Taking her stance in front of the man who might be her father and Ari, she unleashed her fury. The bot began to fire. A wave emitted from Helia's hand, scattering the artillery. The air bent and passed over the bot — the scope shattered, and sparks flew from its circuits. Helia and the bot dropped to the ground in unison.

Ari ran to Helia as the man began to stir.

"Are you okay?"

Helia's eyes were slits. She smiled. "Did I get it?" she asked, looking back at the crumpled pile of metal. Ari met Helia's eyes and smiled back. "And you said this was a suicide mission," Helia said weakly, the corners of her mouth turning into a smirk.

CLANG!

Ari's eyes widened. The sound of hard metal against hard metal pierced their victory. There were more. The robotic steps loudened. Helia's smirk turned to a frown.

"Guess I spoke too soon," Helia whispered.

"What do I do?" Ari pleaded.

Helia knew Ari couldn't defeat the bots alone. The mission *was* suicide. They had failed. Her eyes fluttered as she looked up at Ari. A pang of guilt hit her. The blast drained her energy, making her helpless. A calmness washed over Helia as she accepted her fate. She looked up at Ari, who was panicked and afraid.

"Grant a girl her dying wish," Helia began.

Tears began to stream down Ari's face. She knew it was over. Helia felt moisture well at the corners of her eyes. Ari nodded in response.

"How about a goodbye kiss?"

Hearing the bot's weaponry power up behind her, Ari looked into Helia's eyes. She lowered her face to kiss Helia, whose soft lips met hers. They pressed together, electricity coursing through Ari. Their tears mingled with a mixture of relief and regret. Ari heard the soldier scream as the sound of artillery roared throughout the chamber.

Ari felt the projectiles collide with the armor on her back, but she didn't pull away from Helia. The electricity of their kiss still crackled throughout her body. The electricity turned into power, forming in her core and spreading throughout her body.

Ari felt invincible. Her lips peeled away from Helia's, and Ari felt an even stronger power. Her anger. She wasn't going to lose Helia without a fight. She launched herself at the bots, hurling her fists into the weak points. She had never felt this strong before. Her skin had become armor. There was a crackling glow surrounding her. She could sense every strike from the unified bots before it happened. She tore through all of them with her bare hands.

***

The soldier rushed to Helia. "Donna!"

"It's Helia." I don't even know your name, she said.

"My name is Franco DeSouza," he replied as he embraced the daughter that he thought was dead. "I never thought I would get to meet you."

"We're still alive?" Helia asked, still unsure about hugging DeSouza back.

DeSouza let go of Helia and looked up. He watched Ari rip through the AE defenses as if she were a toddler in a berserk tantrum, destroying toys in a rage. DeSouza looked back at Helia and nodded.

"We're alive. Is Donna?" DeSouza asked, afraid of the answer.

A faint smile passed Helia's face. "She's safe in the Freelands."

"I have to see her!"

"We have to get out of here first."

"What do I need to do?" DeSouza asked with newfound determination.

"Grab the key fob in the bag. Find the central console. That virus will give us control and lock out anyone else."

DeSouza scrambled to the bag. He rummaged and found the key fob.

***

Controller St. Jean watched, cursing, as he witnessed the AE defenses fail. The guards eyed each other anxiously. St. Jean's shoulders dropped. He knew what he had to do. Scorched-earth protocol. Cincuenta Yuno would be leveled, but it wouldn't fall into the hands of Mutie scum.

Knowing their families would be lost if the Controller's plan went to the next stage, the two bodyguards grabbed St. Jean before he could launch the command.

"What are you doing?"

"We can't let you destroy the city, sir," one of the guards responded.

"This is treason! Do you know what it means if we let the Mutie scum get control? You're jeopardizing our way of life!"

"At least our children will live to see it, sir."

***

DeSouza rushed through the scattered piles of smoking metal. Key fob in hand, DeSouza located the central console. A dated monochromatic screen blinked. DeSouza found a port and inserted the key fob. The screen flickered to life, and a string of code ran across it. DeSouza's eyes returned to the elevator. Helia had made it to her feet. She was hobbling onto the battlefield, surveying the destruction the Mule had left behind.

***

Helia couldn't believe what she was seeing. How could Ari levy such destruction? She looked into the massive outpost and saw DeSouza standing at a console not too far away. He had carried out his task and was watching her with wonder. It was all too surreal for Helia, but she could feel DeSouza was fighting the same internal struggle — joy, disbelief, hope. Helia found Ari stomping on the last bot, her strong frame glowing with power. *This is new,* Helia thought. Ari looked up. Their eyes met, and Ari rushed to her.

Helia asked, "What was that?"

Ari shrugged. Her strong hands gripped Helia's. "Are you okay?"

Helia nodded. "Do you know how you did that?"

Ari shook her head, somewhat embarrassed at her show of raw aggression. The last crackles of electricity left Ari's eyes. Helia smiled. She had an idea. "Thank you for saving me. Again." Helia pulled Ari into her.

As their lips met, Ari felt the rush of energy return.

Helia pulled away and noticed Ari's eyes alight. "There it is again. This is exciting."

Ari beamed back at her.

DeSouza motioned to Helia. "This feels as good a time as any to introduce myself to your partner here. I'm Franco DeSouza. Thank you for keeping my daughter safe."

"Ari," she said, offering her hand to shake. Ari cast a knowing look at Helia that she would *always* be there to keep her safe.

Helia could sense the lingering guilt and regret coming from her father. The joy and hope were stronger, though.

A noise from the other side of the consoles made them jump. Officers in lab coats emerged.

"We aren't armed! We aren't against you!" one of the science officers called.

Helia was still recovering from the blast. But even from here, their scent was palpable. They weren't a threat. They were scared. It was clear they weren't here working by choice. That didn't evoke much sympathy from Helia after what they had done, but she focused on the bigger picture.

Helia gave them a halfhearted wave, turned back to the console, and removed the key fob. "It seems to have worked." She wouldn't truly know if they had control until she reported back to Troy. This felt right, though.

"How did you do that with those bots?" DeSouza asked Ari, who just shrugged again. She wasn't used to being the center of attention. The science officers had moved closer and overheard DeSouza's question. They began peppering Ari with similar questions. Ari broke free and returned to Helia's side.

"We did it! I don't believe it!" Ari whispered.

Helia wrapped her arm around her with a twinkle in her eye. "I was never worried."

"What now?" Ari asked with genuine excitement.

"Back to base. The Freelands." Helia paused.

Ari sensed she wouldn't like what came next. "What?" she pleaded.

"Well, until we receive further orders," Helia said with a grin.

Ari's shoulders slumped, and Helia laughed.

"You didn't want this to be over so quickly, did you?"

Ari perked up, matching Helia's elation. "Well, maybe the throngs of people trying to kill us part."

"Sorry, hon, I don't think I can promise that."

Helia felt content. She was on her way home with her new family. A future finally full of promise.

The End

ACKNOWLEDGEMENTS

Thank you so much for reading *The Mutant and the Mule*. Your readership means the world to me, and I hope you enjoyed the journey as much as I enjoyed writing it. This story wouldn't have reached you without a lot of help along the way, and I'd like to take a moment to express my gratitude.

First and foremost, I owe so much to my wife, Sarah, and our children, Nathan and Miranda. Your unwavering support and encouragement have been my foundation. You give me the space and inspiration to pursue my writing passions, and for that, I am eternally grateful.

I also want to extend my deepest thanks to my editors, Ellie Nalle and Hilary Wright. Your expertise and dedication brought my characters and story to life in ways I could only dream of. Your contributions have been invaluable.

Finally, a heartfelt thank you to Histria Books and Diana Livesay. Your belief in my work and your ongoing support have been instrumental in helping my stories reach readers. I am truly grateful for everything you do to support authors like me.

Thank you all for being part of this journey.

Other fine books available from Histria SciFi & Fantasy:

  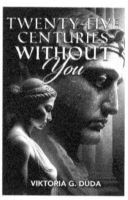

For these and many other great books visit
HistriaBooks.com